The Witch Family

by Eleanor Estes

THE MOFFATS

THE MIDDLE MOFFAT

RUFUS M.

THE HUNDRED DRESSES

THE SLEEPING GIANT

GINGER PYE
(Newbery Medal Winner)

A LITTLE OVEN

PINKY PYE

THE WITCH FAMILY

THE ALLEY

MIRANDA THE GREAT

THE LOLLIPOP PRINCESS

THE TUNNEL OF HUGSY GOODE

The Witch Family

ELEANOR ESTES

Illustrated by Edward Ardizzone

A VOYAGER/HBJ BOOK

HARCOURT BRACE JOVANOVICH

NEW YORK AND LONDON

Library of Congress Catalog Card Number: 60-11250
Printed in the United States of America
ISBN 0-15-298574-3

L M N O P

For
R.
and
H.
and
M.S.
and
W.
and
M.
and
P.
and
Y
O
U

Contents

1   OLD WITCH, BANISHED   13

2   LITTLE WITCH GIRL   23

3   MALACHI, THE BUMBLEBEE   33

4   THE WITCH SCHOOL   42

5   LITTLE WITCH GIRL's BIRTHDAY PARTY   55

6   IN A "HAUNCHED" HOUSE   63

7   THE MERMAID LAGOON   76

8   THE BABY WITCH   87

9   THE PAINTING FIELD   98

10   DANGER IN THE PAINTING FIELD   106

11   THE PICNIC AT THE MERMAID LAGOON   115

12   THE SPELLING BEE   123

13   THE GREAT NIGHT AT LAST   135

14   HALLOWEEN ON GARDEN LANE   143

15   THE REAL WITCH AND THE PRETEND WITCH   149

16   A RIDE ON A BROOMSTICK   159

17   MALACHI, TO THE RESCUE   166

18   GRASS!   176

The Witch Family

CHAPTER ONE

Old Witch, Banished

One day, Old Witch, the head witch of all the witches, was banished. Amy, just an ordinary real girl, not a witch, said Old Witch would have to go away. So, Old Witch had to go. Instead of living in the briers and the brambles, the caves and the heaths, instead of flying around on her broomstick wherever she wanted, chanting runes, doing abracadabras, casting spells and hurly-burlies, this great-great (multiply the "great" by about one hundred and you have some idea of how old she was) old grandmother Old Witch had to go and live on the top of an awful, high, lonely, bare, bleak, and barren glass hill! And at first, she had to live in the witch house up on that hill all alone because at first there was no witch family—there was just herself.

She had to go and live on the bare glass hill because Amy, appalled at the wickedness of the old witch, had said she must. Amy was almost seven, and she had a friend, Clarissa, who was almost seven too. They both had blond hair that hung straight and long, and they both had blue eyes. Amy's blond hair was the color of moonlight. Clarissa's was the color of sunlight. They might have been sisters, they looked so much alike. But they were not sisters. They were best friends, and they were both in the same class in Jasper School.

They were both brave girls. Clarissa could go all the way to the library alone. And although Amy did not yet go to the library alone, she was a brave girl too, for she did not mind booster shots. Moreover, it was she who had the bravery to think it up and say, "Go!" to the mean old wicked old witch.

Amy and Clarissa lived three doors apart on a beautiful street named Garden Lane. Ginkgo trees, meeting high overhead, lined the street on both sides. This street was in the city of Washington, D.C. Clarissa's house was a small brick one painted light pink. It had a square front porch, where she and Amy, on hot days, sometimes had lunch, usually long "noodoos"—a name that Clarissa had long ago, when she was quite small, given to spaghetti, a name that in Clarissa's family, and in Amy's too, had stuck through the years. Or sometimes Amy and Clarissa just sat there on the front porch and ate popsicles and talked and watched the passers-by.

But usually they played in Amy's house. Amy's house was a high red brick one. In front of it there was a tall and graceful ginkgo tree whose roots made the worn red bricks of the sidewalk bulge and whose branches fanned the sky. The ginkgo tree has little leaves shaped like fans that Amy and Clarissa liked to press and give to their dolls. The fruit of this tree is orange, but it is not good for eating. It has an odd fragrance that grownups do not like but that children do not mind, for it makes them think of fall and Halloween.

Near Amy's front stoop there was a small fir tree to which Amy had tied a fragile rope swing. It was a very little swing, but it was strong enough for Amy and Clarissa, each one of these girls weighing only thirty-eight pounds so far. Frequently, while Amy was at Jasper School, Bear or the doll, Patricia, was allowed to sit in this swing all morning. And swinging there on summer days, Amy or Clarissa could keep track of the bees that nested in the bare ground of the yard where the ivy did not grow.

But now it was wintertime. There were no bees in the front yard to watch, though there was one ancient hoary bee—it was hard to tell whether he was dead or alive—in a sunny corner of the back yard. This was a bumblebee.

Amy and Clarissa always had a great deal to do. They both loved to draw pictures, and, seated opposite each other at Amy's little yellow table in her mother's big front bedroom, high up behind the ginkgo tree, they were drawing pictures now, pictures of witches.

It was cold late February, not Halloween. But at lunchtime, while Amy was eating her lamb chop, and Clarissa was standing by watching her eat it bite by bite—she had already had her long "noodoos"—Amy's mother had told a story about Old Witch. Summer, spring, winter, fall, Amy loved to hear stories about Old Witch. "One day, Old Witch . . ." Mama always began.

And that was the way she had begun today, and had then told an awful, though not too awful, story about Old Witch, with many interruptions and suggestions from Amy.

That is why now, after lunch, Amy and Clarissa, having Old Witch very much on their minds, happened to be drawing pictures of her.

"Go, go, go! To the glass hill go!" Amy sang as she drew. She looked closely at her picture for a moment. "You

go!" she repeated firmly. "And never come back!" she said with finality as she banished Old Witch.

"Go," echoed Clarissa. "To the glass hill, go!"

"Don't put any flowers on it!" said Amy. "Nothing grows on this awful bare glass hill. It is all glass, just plain glass. Up there there are no trees, no flowers, no violets. There is plain nothing."

"Nothing," said Clarissa, chewing the end of her crayon thoughtfully.

"The only food that Old Witch can eat is what she can get by magic," declared Amy. "And her magic will not work very well on this shiny place. You know, witch magic works best in dark and gloom. And she can't have any little rabbits to eat at all. You know that rabbits are what she loves best to eat? Don't you, Clarissa?"

"Oh yes," said Clarissa.

"She can have only herbs to eat," said Amy.

"Yes," said Clarissa. "Herb soup morning, noon, and night."

"And the only thing that she can take with her is Old Tom, the awful old black cat, the real head witch cat," declared Amy, going on with the banishment orders. "Oh yes, and her awful old broomstick. And *that's all!*"

At first Amy and Clarissa felt pleased over the banishment of the mean old witch. "I banquished her," said Amy proudly. Sometimes Amy joined two words together, creating one new word. Here, banish and vanquish had become "banquish." "I banquished her," she said. Then she became thoughtful. Doubt swept over her. "It is all right not to have wicked Old Witch most of the year," she thought. "But what about Halloween?"

"Clarissa," she said, "what use is Halloween without the real, right, regular old witch?"

Clarissa clasped her head between her hands, rolled her eyes, and said, "No good!"

"It would be like Christmas without Santa Claus," said Amy.

"And Easter without the Bunny," said Clarissa.

"Same thing," said Amy. "I have to change the order," she said. "Change it to be that Old Witch must stay on top of the glass hill always except for Halloween. She can come down for Halloween. No other time."

"Yes," said Clarissa.

"On Halloween she can ride her broomstick down the glass hill instead of just around the top of it. But only on that one night, can't she, Clarissa?"

"O.K.," said Clarissa.

"If," said Amy, in an ominous voice, "she can learn to be good, that is."

"Yes, of course," said Clarissa.

"Not eat any little rabbits."

"No," said Clarissa.

"Not try to come down off the glass hill at any other time *at all*," said Amy.

"No," said Clarissa.

"You mean, 'yes,'" said Amy.

"Yes," said Clarissa, drawing.

After this change of rule had been decided upon, Amy and Clarissa put away their drawings of witches and went outdoors to the square little back yard. Though the back yard was tiny, still it was big enough to hold Amy's jungle gym with its two swings and glider.

Today was a crisp and sunny day. In summer and in winter the back yard was shaded by a high and lovely linden tree in the corner of the back yard of the house next door, belonging to Polly and Christopher Knapp. Polly Knapp was eight, and she was Amy's and Clarissa's next best friend. Polly let Amy and Clarissa climb her high linden tree in her yard whenever they liked. And Polly, in turn, could swing on Amy's swings and glide on her glider whenever she liked. But she must not go too high and she must never swing on the fragile rope swing in the little fir tree in the front yard because she weighed forty-seven pounds. Neither could Christopher, who was nine, because he weighed sixty-five pounds.

Clarissa got into one of the swings now and started to swing. Amy stood aside for a moment, thinking. In the sunny corner of the yard where Amy was standing dwelled the huge, old, hoary, weather-beaten bumblebee. Amy had discovered him just a few days ago. She had told her father about him. "What is a good name for a bumblebee?" she'd asked.

"Malachi," her father had answered without a second thought. So Amy called the bumblebee, Malachi.

There he was now, basking in the sunshine. Some might have thought that he was dead, for he never moved and summer was gone. But Amy knew that Malachi was just sleeping. "Bumblebees do sleep with their eyes open," she told Clarissa.

"Hello," said Amy to Malachi gently. He did not stir or wink an eye. So Amy swung herself onto the green board fence and up into Polly Knapp's linden tree.

Suddenly dark clouds swept over the sun. "It must be Old Witch going," thought Amy. She looked down at Clarissa. "Did you hear a little thunder?" she asked.

"No," said Clarissa.

"I did. Just a little in the distance. You do not have to be afraid. Probably Old Witch is on her way. Tell her the change in the banquishment order," said Amy. "Tell her she can come down for Halloween! That's all."

Clarissa laughed gaily. She was not afraid of Old Witch. The wind was in her face and her hair whipped against her cheeks. "All right," she said. And, "Hey, wait a minute, Old Witch," she yelled bravely. "Amy says you can come down for Halloween. That's all!"

"Yes, yes! Just Halloween!" repeated Amy. Amy also felt quite brave, having heard herself spoken of as the one in charge. And besides, though there were no leaves at this time of year on the linden tree, she thought she might be invisible to the Old Witch.

Suddenly from the dark clouds a few drops of rain fell.

Amy shivered. She thought she heard the rustling of Old
Witch's black robes. She thought they brushed against her
hair as Old Witch, enraged but truly invisible, steered her
broomstick upward toward the glass hill, going where she
had to go—up, up, and up the awful, bare, and faraway
hill. Amy thought, too, that she heard the buzzing, foreboding sound of a bumblebee.

"Did you hear a bumblebee?" she asked Clarissa.

"No, I heard no bumblebee," said Clarissa.

The sun came out again, which proved that Old Witch
had really gone. Wind and rain had stopped. Amy came
back from the other side of the huge trunk of the linden
tree where she had hidden herself in case Old Witch, out of
revenge, should try to cast a spell on her. "Clarissa. Do you
know what I am going to do?" she said. "I am going to
write Old Witch a letter so she will understand not to come
back at any time except Halloween. She might not have
heard. You must always put things in writing; you know
that, don't you?"

Amy loved to write letters. "I don't know why I like to
write letters. I just do," she confided. Clarissa said she did
not like to. She still owed her grandmother in Tangiers a
letter from two Christmases ago. If she could only get it
written! "Can't you write that thank-you letter?" That's
what her mother said with a sigh several times a year.

Climbing down from the tree, Amy jumped into her
yard. It was very sunny and warm now that Old Witch
had gone. This was the sort of day that Malachi loved. Amy
went over to say good-by to him. But ah-h . . . now,
from his sunny corner, Malachi was gone!

Amy stood there, looking at the place where he used to
live and musing. "I thought I heard a bumblebee," she

thought. Supposing Old Witch should cast a spell on him?

"Do you think Old Witch would hurt Malachi, eat him, even? In some places people do eat bees," she said to Clarissa.

"Oh no," said Clarissa. "She wants to be sure she can come down for Halloween, you know."

"Of course," said Amy.

They went in, took off their warm winter coats, and sat down again at Amy's little yellow table. Instead of drawing, this time Amy wrote the letter to Old Witch. When she did not know how to spell words, she made them up. She knew that made-up words would not matter to Old Witch, for witches are accustomed to doing everything backward and forward and backward again, and if there are too many or too few letters in a word, they do not care —unless they have to be in a spelling bee, of course.

"Now," said Amy, when she had finished. "Listen to this."

Clarissa tried to listen.

Amy read:

"Dear great-great-grandmother Old Witch,
You must be good. You must not be bad. You must go and live on the glass hill always. But if you will be good, you can come back on Halloween night. So, please be good!" (And then Amy signed the letter the way she signed all her letters.)

"I love you and you love me,

Amy.

P.S. Did you take Malachi, the bumblebee?

A."

When this letter was all tightly folded up, it was just a little wad of a note. Amy opened the middle window and put it on the sill. Right away, a red cardinal bird, handsome and sparkling in the winter sun, alighted on the sill. He took the little letter in his bill, and away he flew with it.

"Did you see that?" Amy asked excitedly. "Clarissa. Did you see that?"

"I did," said Clarissa.

"It would be as good as finding a letter in a bottle in the ocean to find a letter in a bird's bill. Don't you think so, Clarissa?" Amy said.

Clarissa nodded. Clarissa was apt not to think that things like notes in birds' bills were as remarkable as Amy did. She took events as they came, not questioning the usualness or the unusualness of them. But Amy was still wonderstruck. She leaned her arms on the window sill and cupped her chin in her hands, and she watched the far distant red streak, the cardinal bird, as it flew over the houses across the street and then up, and up, and up, and away.

"Good-by," called Amy from the window. "Don't lose it!" she said.

What a morning! Old Witch banished. Malachi gone. And a bird with a note in his bill. Exhausted, Amy lay down on the big bed. Clarissa put on the record, "How Much Is That Doggie in the Window?" She sat in Amy's little red rocker and listened, and rocked, and nodded.

CHAPTER TWO

Little Witch Girl

One day, Old Witch was rocking in her wicker rocker on the creaky front porch of the witch house. She was not happy, and she was brooding. She did not like it up here on this bare, bleak glass hill. When she stepped off the porch, she slipped. Her feet went out from under her, for the glass was like ice. She looked like a very bad ice skater, and Old Tom laughed at the silly sight she made trying to regain her balance. No one else would have laughed, for Old Witch, banished or not, might angrily have cast a spell. However, Old Tom would not have minded being cast in a spell. Though he was a witch cat, Tom was as curious about everything, including awful spells, as an ordinary cat.

"Tluck, tluck, tluck," muttered Old Witch. "How dismal it is up here! All this sunshine glinting on the glass. No brambles, no briers! No wilderness to put a foot in! No swamps!" Old Witch pulled her peaked hat down over her eyes and sulked. She pined for the company of another witch, even though all other witches were of less importance than she.

"Oh, to glory be! It's terrible," she said to Old Tom. "Where is the rhyme and reason," she asked, "of being good all the time, as *her* instructed when *her* banquished me (she said "banished" the way Amy did), all by myself and with none to clap?"

"Nobby," Old Tom reminded her in a rusty, rasping voice. (Nobby was the real name of this famous old witch.) "*I'm* here," he said.

"I was referring to witches, not cats, however talented," Old Witch replied.

"Once I was a witch," thought Old Tom, cleaning a paw. "I am a graduated witch." But Old Tom did not remind Old Witch of the fact that witches turn into cats when they go into retirement. And pretending to doze, Tom turned his eyes to the other end of the porch where something, a bumblebee in hiding, sometimes engaged his attention.

Old Witch thought no more about Old Tom. Cats sometimes watch a speck of dust, or even nothing, for hours. "How dull!" thought Old Witch. But dull as life was on this awful glass hill, Old Witch had to bear it. She had to be good, not good in the way witches enjoy being good—that is in casting wicked spells and eating up little rabbits whenever they have the chance—but good in the way that real regular people are good—that is in *not* casting spells and *not* eating up little rabbits every minute. Though she drooled terribly for a taste of rabbit, her favorite food—rabbits and their painted eggs—she was good. She ate her herb soup daily, and she made no attempt to escape from this place of "banquishment." Otherwise, Amy said, she would not be able to have a hurly-burly even on Halloween!

For this difficult goodness, Old Witch received a reward. As she sat unhappily rocking, she got a second letter. The same beautiful red cardinal bird who had brought her the first letter brought this one too, tightly folded up in a wad in his bill. It, too, was from Amy, the banisher, on Garden Lane.

"Quite a pen pal, she are," said Old Witch, half sarcastically, half fondly. She read the letter out loud with an audience of—she thought—just Tom. So far she had not suspected the presence of the bumblebee.

"Dear mean old wicked Old Witch,

When you wake up in the morning, sing an abracadabra (you know the one that goes, Abracadabra, A B C . . .), close your eyes, and then open them again, and you *might* have company.

> I love you and you love me,
> Amy.

P.S. You never answered about Malachi, the bumblebee. Did you take him? I don't mean *steal*. I mean *take*, by *mistake*, the day you flew away. He disappeared that day. Please shake out your shawl and see. Love, A."

"Oh, to glory be!" exclaimed Old Witch. "Company! Did you hear that, Nobby?" (She sometimes talked to herself.) Old Witch read the letter again. "What bumblebee named Malachi is she harping on, anyway? I haven't any of her old bumblebees." But to make certain, Old Witch shook out her black shawl, and there was no bumblebee in it. Old Witch hoped that Amy's promise of company did not mean a bumblebee, even though beeswax is excellent in magic and necromancy. "But when," she asked herself, "on this awful place, would there be need for beeswax in magic? No need," she answered herself. What she really wanted was some sort of witch for company, not

some sort of bumblebee. "Malachi," she muttered. "A portentous name," she had to grant. Carefully she studied Amy's letter anew.

Old Tom again turned his eyes to the sunniest corner of the creaky front porch. He knew that there, in his new dwelling, Malachi had hidden himself. Being at this season a dusty, faded, tawny color, Malachi blended with the weather-beaten woodwork and was camouflaged. Nevertheless, Old Tom had known about Malachi's presence from the start, for cats' eyes detect much that the eyes of

wicked old witches do not. Malachi was safe from Tom,
however. Cats are fond of crickets, not of bumblebees
whose fuzz and fur stick in their throats, and whose stings
they must beware of besides. Tom liked the idea of there
being something up here for him to watch, something Old
Witch did not know about. "I know something you don't
know," his sly eyes seemed to say.

Her curiosity aroused by Amy's letter, Old Witch
looked in the index of her huge book of runes under Malachi and under bumblebee. She found nothing of value.
However, she did come upon some clippings that she had
garnered through the years from the Witch Gazette, stuck
loosely in the book, like recipes in cookbooks. Among these
clippings she found an ancient, crumbly, yellow-edged
rune that might have a bearing on the special bumblebee in
question. She read it aloud.

> "Oh, Malachi,
> Oh, Malachi,
> You are a magic
> bumblebee.
> If in trouble
> e'er I be,
> Then mumble,
> bumble,
> here to me."

There were several versions of this incantation. Another
version read,

> "Malachi,
> Oh, Malachi,
> You are the
> spelling bumble*bye*,

> You are the
> spelling bumble*bee*
> Of everything
> From A to Z.
> And if in trouble
> e'er I be,
> then mumble,
> bumble,
> here to me."

In this way, without knowing one thing about it, by reciting these runes aloud, Old Witch cast a magic spell on Malachi. Now, in his new dwelling, he basked in magic. To look at him, he appeared no different than he had when basking in his sunny corner in Amy's little back yard on Garden Lane. Yet now he had been touched by witch magic. And, he could spell.

"T H A N K S," he spelled right now, practicing.

He spoke so softly that Old Witch did not hear him. Little suspecting what she had done and having resolved to pay no heed to the matter of Malachi, which she judged to be a child's fancy, Old Witch went into her house, prepared her herb soup, and went to bed. She was impatient for morning to come. For a long time she lay awake wondering if the company to which Amy referred could mean her old rival, Famous Green Caterpillar Witch. Even she would be better than no one, she thought. At last she fell asleep.

When morning came, Old Witch followed Amy's instructions. She chanted her abracadabra song, which is a secret song, but which goes somewhat like this:

> "Abracadabra
> A B C

Flying through the air to me
Hotch
Cotch
In the Potch
Who is this that I do see?"

She sang rustily, for, except to get herbs, she had not had much occasion to use magic in her exile on this hill. Nevertheless, the abracadabra worked with prompt success. After all, this witch was still Head Witch of all witches whether she had been banished to the top of a glass hill or not. And when, according to instructions, she opened her eyes, what did she see?

A little witch girl of exactly the same size as Amy and Clarissa, and of the same age, too—almost seven—that is what she saw! She came with a little black witch cloak and a tall, peaked little black witch hat. Her thin, black-clad legs were flung casually over her small witch broomstick, and a wobbly little black kitten, miaowing menacingly, was clinging to the broom end of the broomstick.

"Oh, to glory be!" gasped Old Witch. This was the last thing that she had expected. A little witch girl had not entered her mind. But it had entered Amy's mind. Otherwise, how could there be a witch family? One witch does not make a family. But now, anyway, there are more— Old Witch, number one; Little Witch Girl, number two; Old Tom, number three; wobbly Little Tommy, number four. And also, don't forget Malachi, magic Malachi, the bumblebee, drowsing in his corner, all covered over with the magic of a rune like pollen from a flower. He—with his three red ruby eyes open as always—is number five of the witch family.

From under her peaked black hat the little witch girl's hair hung long and blond and straight, very unusual in a witch.

"B E H O L D!" spelled a voice from the end of the porch. Old Witch gave a start but decided to ignore the intrusion. She sank back on her haunches. She was exhausted from the difficult abracadabra she had performed and weak with wonder at the dazzling spectacle of a beautiful fairhaired little witch girl. She cupped her long curved chin in the nobby palms of her hands, and she looked long and hungrily at Little Witch Girl—not hungrily in the manner that she might have in the old times before she had been "banquished" and was still a mean old bad Old Witch, but hungrily in the new way, for love and company.

"Hello," she said with a croak to the little witch girl.

"Hello," answered the little witch girl with the merest, slightest suspicion of a tiny, charming croak in her own voice.

"Be ye Malachi?" asked Old Witch. "Be ye" seemed the correct language to use to such a pretty girl. "Be ye Malachi, or whatever that name be that *her* keeps harping on?"

"Malachi!" The little witch girl laughed. "Of course not. He's a bumblebee. Oh, I get it. You thought that I was a bumblebee in disguise. Well, I'm not. My name is Hannah, and I am a plain witch."

"Welcome," said Old Witch affably. "I'm glad you are not an old bumblebee!"

The little witch girl made herself at home and examined everything. She flew inside, and with her in it, the house did not look bleak any more. It still looked shabby and old, but it did not look ugly. She flew back outside. "What a beautiful place this is," she exclaimed, "all so shiny and slippery!"

The sun was rising. Beautiful colors, rose, pink, gold, and violet, were reflected in the glass hill. The top of the hill, where the witch house was, seemed to float above the rosy-tipped clouds. Even Old Witch was impressed, though black, naturally, was her favorite color. "Oh, to glory be!" she said.

The clouds began to lift. Little Witch Girl stared way way off in the distance. Far away she could see a blue line, the horizon, the edge of the ocean.

"I like the porch. I like the view," said the little witch girl. "But where's my rocker, my red rocker? And where's my bed?"

"I didn't know you were coming." Old Witch apologized. "Or I'd have had a bed and a rocker. They're coming, though. Wait . . . just wait . . ."

A slow smile spread over Old Witch's face. "They'll be coming, the rocker and the bed," she said with a soft croak. But to herself, she said, "At least I *hope* they'll be coming." Would her abracadabra work for her again? She tried very hard, and it did work. With her abracadabra, incantations, runes, and chants, Old Witch got the following necessities for the little witch girl: a little red rocker that played a tune when you rocked in it (the tune was, "Little Witch, Little Witch, A-born in a Ditch"), a little brass bed with small brass owls carved on the four posts, and a little black brush and comb.

Brush and comb? A necessity? It is against witch rules to take off hats and brush and comb hair. Was Old Witch going to disobey witch rules concerning hair?

A slight buzzing sound could be heard to which Old Witch paid no heed as she recklessly seized the brush and the comb and grabbed hold of the little witch girl.

"DONT!" spelled a buzzing voice sharply in her ear. This voice skipped the apostrophe. Otherwise the spelling was perfect.

CHAPTER THREE

Malachi, the Bumblebee

As before, Old Witch heard the word of Malachi, but again she paid no heed. Witches never comb their hair, and many even sleep in their hats. This would not be comfortable for us, but witches do not mind, for it is the custom never to take off peaked hats. Even Amy, who knew this rule about witches always having to keep their peaked hats on and who may have made the rule up along with the banishment, had never drawn witches with their hats off—always with hats on. Old Witch, herself, had never taken off her own hat and combed her own hair, but she had decided to brush and comb Hannah's hair, for she had never seen anything as soft and pretty. Though witches do not comb their own hair, they hanker to get their hands into other people's. Remember Rapunzel! And how the old witch in that story liked to comb and comb Rapunzel's hair! Of course Little Witch Girl's hair was not as long as Rapunzel's famous hair, but it was lighter in feeling. Old Witch was determined to get her hands into it as soon as possible. She threw Hannah's hat on the bed and she began to comb.

The buzzing grew loud again, and it sounded ominous. Old Witch brushed her hand around her head as though to shoo something away, but she continued to break the witch rule—never to comb witch hair.

"Stop that!" cried the little witch girl angrily. She did not like to have her hair combed and to break witch rules. "Stop that!" she cried again. "That hurts!" she said. "Don't you hear Malachi?"

"S T O P!" spelled the bee.

"Ouch!" said Old Witch. She dropped the comb. Something had stung her on the wrist. Being magic now, Malachi, unlike ordinary bees who have but one stinger, had refill stingers, and the minute he used up one, another stinger popped into place. Being much larger than most bumblebees, he had an extra cell for stinger refills as many pencils do for lead. The little witch girl broke away and crawled under her little brass bed. She stayed there, peeking out, until Old Witch promised to comb no more. Then Little Witch Girl crept out. She put the brush and comb way, way under the bed, and she sat down and watched Old Witch suspiciously.

Old Witch was puzzled. She sucked her bee bite, and she studied it carefully. A bee had stung her and she could not see the bee. She shook out her shawl. There was no bee in it or on her or anywhere around, for Malachi, his warning having been heeded, had returned to his crumbly groove in the ancient board in the sunny part of the porch. From his place of camouflage, his watchful, anxious eyes did not relax their vigil.

The little witch girl was still indignant. Her feelings were very ruffled. "Do you want me to catch cold?" she asked Old Witch. She put her hat back on, went outdoors, sat down in her red rocker, turned the music off, and rocked silently.

After a while she felt better and she said, "Thank you for the presents. We are not up to the abracadabra for red rockers in school yet. We are only up to easy ones like getting a bird's feather" (Old Witch croaked gently in encouragement. "That's good," she said), "a happy toad, and a milk pod. Next week, in witchiplication, we are going to take up harder ones."

Old Witch nodded.

"Want to see me get a feather? I'll try for two feathers, one for your cat and one for my cat."

Old Witch nodded again. Her cat, Old Tom, fixed the newcomer witch with his green eye. He had one yellow eye and one green eye, and it is the green eye of a witch cat that fixes. "Why only the feather of the bird?" this green eye seemed to ask.

Little Witch Girl did not mind being fixed by the green eye of Old Tom or by the green eye of Little Tommy, either. Tommy was learning fast from the old cat, and he fixed his green eye here, there, and particularly at the sunny end of the porch, though he did not know, being so young, that he was looking at the place where there was a magic bee.

In her sweet, rather husky voice, the little witch girl said an abracadabra, keeping time to the chant with her rocking. She had to start several times because abracadabras are like safety locks. If you do not know the right combination, the abracadabra will not work properly and you may get the wrong thing. Finally, Little Witch Girl got the abracadabra right, and she produced two beautiful bright red feathers, a long one for Old Tom and a tiny one for Little Tommy.

Little Tommy played happily with his feather while Old

Tom sniffed his and twitched his tail and reminisced about
birds. Naturally, no birds dwelled up on this high glass hill
where nothing grew. In fact, the only bird ever seen up
here was Amy's emissary, the red cardinal bird. He passed
by the glass hill every day on his way to and from Mount
Rose Park, across the street from Jasper School, where he
went for food. He liked his reflection in the glass hill and
was obliged to come this way, anyway, in case there was a
special message from or to Amy.

"Did you see that?" the little witch girl asked Old
Witch proudly. "I got those feathers."

"That's very good," said Old Witch. "You did very
nicely." She paused a moment, and then she said cannily,
"Since you did so well with the feathers, how about something harder? Be ye interested in trying your hand at the
abracadabra for getting me a . . . bumblebee, say?"

Little Witch Girl shook her head. "Oh, no," she said. "I
be not."

Feeling happier and more at home now, Little Witch
Girl turned the music part of her rocker back on, and she
peacefully sat and rocked.

Old Witch could not take her eyes off the little witch
girl. She was quite overcome at her good fortune. She had
not realized that she was *that* lonely, that her incantations
would bring her a little witch girl for company. "Oh, to
glory be!" she said with a happy hoarse croak. Now she
would never be lonesome on this glassy hill. She thought
up ways to amuse the little witch.

"How about a race around the top of the hill on our
broomsticks?" she asked.

The little witch girl was delighted. So, around and
around the top of the hill the old witch and the little witch,

with their cats astride their broomsticks, flew and raced. Old Witch let Little Witch Girl win every race. This shows what a good person Old Witch was becoming.

But when the races were over, and the big and the little witch had come to a breathless stop on the rickety front porch, the little witch girl was rather scared at the way Old Witch croaked, "Heh-heh! Oh, the hurly-burly!" And she was still more scared when Old Witch danced a fast jig known as "the backanally." This is a real witch dance, and Old Witch danced it all around the little witch girl, who looked straight ahead at the horizon and pretended not to see. But, as the dance went on, she became more and more scared, for whether she looked at Old Witch or not, she could not help but see a great deal of the backanally dance.

She cried, "Stop that!" and ran inside and crawled under her new brass bed again. Such a very little witch was still quite unaccustomed to backanally dances.

A certain forbidding buzzing sound could be heard again. But Old Witch did not hear it because she was singing so loudly. Once in a while she hopped higher into the air suddenly, as though she had been bitten. But she did not care.

"I'll be good! Oh, I'll be good!" she kept on singing. Little Witch Girl stayed right under the bed because the way Old Witch said "good" was enough to scare her stiff. It sounded like "good" in the witch meaning, not "good" in the way that Amy had ordered. The better the witch, from the witch point of view, the worse she is from our point of view and must be banished to glass hills. That's what Amy said.

For a moment Old Witch was mixed up. She had forgotten which "good" she was supposed to be. With her awful

"heh-hehs" she certainly did not sound "good" in our way. But when Old Witch saw the little witch girl take refuge under the bed again and heard—in a lull in the dance—the loud buzzing of the bee, she realized her mistake. She knew that she must not frighten Little Witch Girl or Amy might take her away again. Amy might send her right back where she came from, wherever that was, and cancel Halloween hurly-burly besides.

As Old Witch thought these reformed thoughts, the buzzing sound grew faint. There were no more sudden stings. She said amiably, "Come out, my dear. That was just the noted dance called 'backanally.' Come. Ride your broomstick. You ride very well. Yes, indeedy."

"Thank you," answered the little witch girl stiffly from under the bed where she lay, leaning on her elbows, looking out. She really had been very frightened at the "backanally." Suddenly, way up here on this bleak glass hill, all alone with Old Witch, the little witch girl felt lonely. What did it matter that Old Witch was Head Witch of all witches? Little Witch Girl still felt lonely. "Thank you," she repeated coolly. "And I am a very sweet little witch," she said as if to reassure herself, "and I never go outside the line in coloring," she said. "And I like to draw pictures," she said. "And don't scare me again!" she said.

"Ah-h-h," said Old Witch in as gentle and admiring a croaky voice as possible. "Ah-h-h, to glory be!" And as quick as a flash she got Little Witch Girl some crayons by abracadabra. Also some paper.

So, the little witch girl came crawling out from under the bed and sat down on the porch in her red rocker to draw pictures. She could rock and draw at the same time. As the day wore on, she became accustomed to the sound of Old Witch and was not scared of her heh-hehs any more.

Watching the little witch girl gradually becoming more at ease, the old witch slyly put forth the suggestion again. "Betwixt now and Halloween," she said, "be ye going to catch that, well, that old biting bumblebee for me, perchance?"

"What be the matter with you anyway?" asked Little Witch Girl. "Always talking about bees. Do you perchance have a bee in your bonnet?"

Old Witch grabbed off her high peaked hat. She had not thought to shake this out. But of course there was no bee in it, and she went into the witch house to prepare some lunch.

Tired of drawing, the little witch girl put aside her picture and picked up Old Witch's "Big Booke of Runes," which she had left on the porch yesterday. Thumbing through it, what should fall out of it and into the little witch girl's lap but the rune concerning Malachi!

Little Witch Girl was an excellent reader, and she read this rune aloud, slowly and softly and with expression.

> "Oh, Malachi,
> Oh, Malachi,
> You are a magic
> bumblebee.
> If in trouble
> e'er I be,
> Then mumble,
> bumble,
> here to me."

She read the other verses too. Thus she added to the magic of Malachi, the bumblebee. A smile spread over the face of the little witch girl. "Old Witch must not have this," she thought. She tucked the important rune in the hem of her cloak for safekeeping. Then she tiptoed over to the sunny end of the porch.

"There ye be!" she said lovingly.

There was no response. Malachi looked like a dried-up,

fuzzy piece of winter wheat. The little witch girl reached her forefinger toward him quite cautiously. He raised his furry black head, looked at her with his three red bumblebee eyes, and spelled aloud, "BE NOT AFRAID. I BE HERE."

"Will you make Old Witch be good?" asked the little witch.

The bumblebee spelled, with emphasis, "YES. I BE THE REPRESENTATIFF OF AMY."

"Amy? Who be that?" asked Little Witch Girl, talking the way the bee did.

"SHE BE THE BANQUISHER," said Malachi.

There the conversation ended. With these long words Malachi had outspelled himself. Being a spelling bee, Malachi ordinarily spoke in sentences of just one word. Instead of saying a word, he spelled it. This took longer, but it was more accurate. And he was an accurate bee. When he spelled "BEE," you knew it was bee and not be.

Although Malachi was a spelling bee, he could not cast spells. He, himself, was under a spell, and that was the important thing. The magic spell that he was under enabled him not to cast spells, but to spell. "Very important, this is, too," said Amy to Clarissa, still at the little yellow table drawing.

"YES," said Clarissa, who knew how to spell too.

CHAPTER FOUR

The Witch School

"Well, Amy," said Clarissa. "That little witch girl that lives on the glass hill, doesn't she go to school? Now that she lives with Old Witch, doesn't she have to go to school?"

Clarissa was seated at one side of the little yellow table, drawing a witch picture. Amy, on the other side of the table, was drawing a witch picture, too. They were both drawing very large pictures, and they did not notice or mind these two large pictures getting in each other's way. They were such good friends, they almost never got cross with each other about anything.

"What?" asked Amy, with her hand cupped behind her ear.

Both Amy and Clarissa had colds, and whenever they had colds, they became a little deaf. "What'd you say?" shouted Amy more loudly.

"School!" shouted back Clarissa. "Didn't she ever have to go to school?"

"Of course she went to school," said Amy. "Of course, she did. You didn't think she just rode her broomstick all day, did you? Growing up to be a nope, did you?" ("Nope" was Amy's word for "dope.") "Of course she went to school, to witch school."

With her head turned almost upside down to see, Clarissa studied Amy's picture. There were a witch schoolroom, a witch schoolteacher, and some little witch schoolgirls in the picture. There were cobwebs, and cauldrons, and crystal gazing balls for all.

"Which is our little witchie?" asked Clarissa.

"She's late," said Amy. "She's going to come flying through the window when she comes. Then there will be seven little witches."

"I see," said Clarissa, and they both went on with their drawings.

Today was the little witch girl's first day of school. And she really was late. It is too bad to be late on the first day, but it was really the fault of Old Witch. Last night, as Old Witch and Little Witch sat rocking before the fire, Old Witch, delighted to have such an appreciative audience, had told the little witch story after story of old days when she was a real, right, regular, wicked Old Witch, before her exile to the glass hill. The stories all ended with, "and then *she* banquished me!"

"Tell more, tell more," Little Witch Girl had begged after each story. "Begin. One night, I . . ."

And so Old Witch had told one more and then one more. So, Little Witch Girl had gone to bed very late. And in the morning, naturally, she did not want to get up. "O-o-oh," she groaned. "Do I have to go to school today? Couldn't I begin tomorrow instead?"

"No," said Old Witch with finality. "You see that red bird coming? Well, you follow that red bird. He goes your way. Good-by, my dearie. Get good marks." And she shoved sleepy little witch girl onto her broomstick and out the door.

"Wait! Wait! Wait for me!" the little witch girl called to the cardinal bird. He was already almost out of sight. Trying to catch up with him, Little Witch Girl missed the right turn-off to the witch school, which is located on a pink cloud. Spurring her broomstick on, the next thing she knew she was far from the glass hill and from witch school. She was on some strange street in some strange city, and she was flying low past the window of a high brick house. Here, she became entangled in the branches of a ginkgo tree. Poised there for a moment, she found herself outside the window of a room where two girls (they were Amy and Clarissa) were drawing pictures, and shouting at each other with their hands behind their ears.

"What pretty witches! What a pretty room!" thought the little witch girl. She had never seen real ordinary girls before, and of course, she did not connect these two girls with the girls who banquish, the girls in the stories that Old Witch had told her last night. She noticed that these two girls did not wear witch hats or any hats. "What sort of a witch school is this where the girls do not wear hats?" she wondered. "Beform school?" she asked herself. ("Beform school" was her way of saying "reform school," as it happened also to be Amy's way.)

"Oh, dear," she thought. "I might have to go to 'beform school' if I don't get to my regular school soon. Or I might have to stand in the corner with my hat off."

Luckily for her, since she did not know the way back, the red cardinal bird came flying along right now, heading for home. Disentangling herself from the ginkgo tree, the little witch girl scratched against the window pane of Amy's house. Amy ran to the window. Then she solemnly said to Clarissa, "Clarissa."

"What?"

"I think I just saw the little witch girl."

"What?" asked Clarissa.

"I said," said Amy, speaking slowly, distinctly, and a little more loudly, "that I just saw the little witch girl, ours, not the other ones, flying past our window."

"Oh-h," said Clarissa. "Can't be. You said she was in school. Where we would be if we didn't have colds—thank goodness, we do."

"Well," said Amy. "I said she was going to fly in late. And that is what she is doing this minute, flying in late. How long do you think it takes to fly from here to witch school on a broomstick? Just that long, that's all."

In her picture Amy quickly drew the little witch girl flying in the schoolroom window, the new little witch girl flying into a new school, alone, and late.

The other witch girls were chanting arithmetic runes. In the middle of one and one, they all stopped and stared. Because Little Witch Girl was new, they were all resolved not to like her. "Imagine coming in late the first day!" they twittered. They all, including the witch teacher, watched Little Witch Girl with cold and critical stares. The names of the six other little witch girls were Tweet, Izzy, Olie, Itch and Twitch, who were twins, and Notesy.

"Fly your broomstick to the broomstick rack," said the witch teacher.

Little Witch Girl did this. "Now," said the teacher, "take your copy stool and sit down, the one behind Olie," she said. "Olie, stand, so that the new witch girl will know where to sit."

Tweet stood up instead of Olie, and Little Witch Girl

put her stool behind hers instead of Olie's. The class twittered at the success of this first joke on the new witch.

"What is your name?" asked the teacher. "Spell it."

"Small h, a, double n, a, capital H," answered the little witch girl, getting it right, for witches spell backwards.

"Where do you live?" asked the teacher.

"With Head Witch Nobby on the glass hill," answered the little witch.

All the witches gasped. In the witch house of exile! They

decided to dislike Little Witch Girl more than ever, for
they knew she must be stuck-up, living with a witch of such
importance.

"Why are you late?" asked the witch teacher.

"I went to the wrong school by mistake," answered Little Witch Girl. She still thought that Amy and Clarissa had
been in a school. She had decided not to mention keeping
late hours last night with Old Witch. The less she men-
tioned the name of Old Witch, Head Witch of all the

witches, the better, she decided, because whenever she did do so, one or another of the witches said, "She brags." Little Witch Girl was indignant. After all she had not asked to live with Old Witch. Somehow or another, by abracadabra, she had simply arrived in the witch house.

"Wrong school!" imitated the others with titters. And although the little witch girl had been in this school for only a few minutes, the other little witch girls were already saying that she would probably have to stay back in school this year, she was such a "nope." Despite being witches, they said "dope" the way Amy did—"nope." As the lessons went on, however, they were forced to change their tune, for Little Witch Girl proved to be very bright.

"First lesson," said the witch teacher, clapping her hands. "Arithmetic," she said. "Do the one and one," she told Little Witch Girl.

Little Witch Girl said,

> "One and one is nothing.
> Two and one is one.
> Three and one is two . . ."

"Right," said the teacher. "She knows it all."

Witches subtract, you see, when we add. And they add when we subtract. They say, "Two take away one is three!" Little Witch Girl got all her numbers right. The other little witch girls did not like this, and held a consultation with heads together. They made a plan. Soon they had a chance to put it into effect.

"Second lesson," said the witch teacher. "Exercise!" she said.

The little witches hopped off their copy stools. The exercise was to stomp ten times around the room, exhale and inhale twenty times, stomp ten times around the room again, this time in the other direction, and then stomp back to their copy stools. Stomping was a favorite game of the little witches. One witch was always chosen to stand in the middle of the room and direct the game, and each one wanted to be the stomp director. "Choose me! Choose me!" they all screamed now. But teacher chose the new little witch girl.

"She'll see what the stomp game is like," said the others, and commenced the stomping. Instead of stomping around the room, they stomped around Little Witch Girl, coming closer and closer to her with each round, stomping right up to her and making a little tish sound at her with their tongues, because she was new, and then stomping away again. This game was refreshing to the little witch girls, but it was very unpleasant to Little Witch Girl herself. However, all through the stomping, Little Witch Girl held tight to the hem of her cloak where a certain important rune was folded up in a wad. She knew the rune by heart, but she liked, nevertheless, to feel it for added courage. So she stood staunch and firm and did not flinch.

"Spelling, next lesson," said the teacher, who had enjoyed the stomping show and had not interfered. To herself she had to admit that, so far, the new pupil had shown herself to be not only bright but brave.

The little witch girls made ready to spell.

"Spell hurly-burly," said the teacher to the little witch girl.

Little Witch Girl spelled it "hulie-bulie," so she got it wrong. This was the only word that she spelled wrong, however, so she was good in this subject also. "Some day," the teacher promised her, "we shall have a spelling bee."

"I have one already," said the little witch girl without thinking.

"Rude. Stand in corner with hat off for five minutes," said the teacher.

Of course, the teacher did not realize that the little witch girl was referring to Malachi, and Little Witch Girl had more sense than to explain. She bore her punishment unflinchingly. During this five minutes the other little witch girls were permitted to stomp again. This teacher believed in plenty of exercise.

Again the little witch girls stomped up to Little Witch Girl, and they pulled her long light hair, and they said they did not like her hair because it was not spiky and black. They tweaked her nose, and they stepped on her toes, trying to make her say, "Ee-eek!" She did not say "Ee-eek!" She remained staunch, and she still did not flinch. But she had had enough of the stomping. Very quietly, she whispered, "Malachi, oh, Malachi," and the rest of the rune.

"Ow, ow!" said the first stomping witch girl. "Something has bitten me."

The same thing happened to each stomping witch girl, and they stopped stomping and tweaking and saying, "Tish!" in Little Witch Girl's face immediately.

"Teacher," complained Olie. "Something bit me!"

"And me," said Tweet.

"And me," said all the others. "Ow-ow," they said. "Something has bitten us." And all returned to their copy stools to compare bites.

The witch teacher peered closely at the little witch girls' hands to see the bites. "I don't see any bites," she said.

"Well, I wish you could feel them," said the rude girl, Olie. Olie had to stand in the corner for five minutes with her hat off for punishment. There she stood, blowing petulantly on her hand.

"Now," said the witch teacher. "Next lesson, witchiplication. And no more complaining about bites or you will all have to stand in the corner with your hats off, that is, all except Hannah," she said. "She has uttered no complaints."

The little witch girls surveyed the newcomer with extreme distaste. "Pet," they croaked.

Witchiplication is a very hard and important subject for witches. It deals with magic. Poison apples, poison brew, love potions, warts—taking them off, and warts—putting them on, things that creep and crawl, forebodings, these were some of the main runes of the subject. It was Little Witch Girl's favorite study, and though it was difficult, she always got A.P. in it, which means absolutely perfect.

The other little witches, nursing their bites, were feeling cross. Little Witch Girl had not got one bite, they noticed. But each one of them got a bite every time she was about to tweak Little Witch Girl's nose or pull her hair. They had not taken in the fact that Little Witch Girl was in charge of the bites, or they would have been more respectful. They certainly would not have tried what they were now about to try. After a whispered consultation, they had resolved to show off their witchiplication and cast spells on Little Witch Girl. They were going to take turns.

First came Olie. She marched thrice around the new little witch girl and sang a throaty, raucous rune. The purpose of this rune was to ensnare the little witch girl in spider webs. But before the spiders came, Little Witch Girl quickly said her counteracting magical Malachi rune. Olie fell back instantly, stung in three places. "Ouch!" she said.

Matters fared no better for the other little witches. The twins, who were the last ones to try to cast a spell on Little Witch Girl, recited a twin witchiplication, called a witchiplication-witchiplication, a powerful one intended just for twins. But, "Ouch! ouch!" they too had to say, having received twin, rather than single, bites all over them.

Then, all the witch girls understood the magical connection between the bites and the new little witch girl. And when they heard a buzzing voice spell the words, "BEE-HOOVES YE TO BEEHAVE," they curtsied in respect.

Little Witch Girl had been sitting very tensely on her little copy stool throughout this ordeal. Now, however, she was absolutely certain that the powerful magic of Malachi was stronger than that of any of the witch girls and that she would be quite safe.

The other little witch girls, all with bites that did not show but that stung nevertheless, now conceived a great admiration for the new girl. They swung completely around. They resolved to put an end to their teasing, to stop their stomping, and they decided to like her, knowing how excellent she was in witchiplication.

"She's brilliant!" they exclaimed, and clapped their hands.

Little Witch Girl stood up, took a bow, and received a double A.P. from the teacher. The teacher appraised the little witch girl with approval. She could see that the new little witch was going to be more than able to take care of herself. Thoughtfully, she examined the bites again that she could not see. "Maybe it's an epidemic," suggested the teacher brightly. "School will have to close."

So, in honor both of the brilliant new pupil and the epidemic of invisible bee bites, she dismissed the class.

The cardinal bird was waiting on the window sill to conduct the little witch girl home. Amy had told him always to do this so that the little witch girl would not get lost again. And now, he sped to the glass hill, leading the way home.

Old Witch, who had spent the morning searching for the lost Malachi rune, to no avail, welcomed her with a snack of herbs. "Well," she said amiably. "How did you make out?"

"Fine," said Little Witch Girl with a yawn.

Then Little Witch Girl sat down in her red rocker and rocked. She thought about the two girls she had seen this morning in the high brick house on Garden Lane. And she thought about school. She wished she could play with those two girls in the window. She was sure that they would not stomp.

"Gammer?" she said. It was her new, affectionate way of speaking to Old Witch.

"Eh?" croaked Old Witch.

"Could I go down to Garden Lane and play with two witch girls I saw down there?"

"What!" croaked Old Witch. You would think Little Witch Girl was deaf with a cold, like Amy and Clarissa, Old Witch screamed so. "What!" she said. "Why they be not witch girls. They be real regular girls. They be Amy and Clarissa, the ones I told you about last night. They be my banquishers! You must not go down there again. Or I may be not able to hurly-burly on Halloween. That's what 'em said, 'em did. Oh, to glory be!"

Old Witch was so upset, her abracadabra worked without her bidding it to. Wind blew and thunder rumbled. Rain and hail also fell. Old Witch was about to do the frightening backanally dance but changed her mind when she received a bite.

Down below, on Garden Lane, Amy and Clarissa put away their drawings.

"That's good," admired Clarissa.

"So's yours," said Amy.

"I see you added a bee and a bird," said Clarissa.

"Yes," said Amy. "The red bird is my missionary. The bumblebee (that's Malachi, the bumblebee—he's gone from the back yard, you know) is my representatiff. I selected him."

Living in Washington, D.C., Amy knew about the House of Representatives, and had even visited it. Also the Senate.

"Your what?" asked Clarissa, putting her hand behind her ear.

"Representatiff!" said Amy clearly.

Suddenly the wind whisked her drawing across the room. "O-o-oh!" she said. "Hear the thunder! That is thunder, isn't it?"

"Yes," said Clarissa. "And hail!" she said.

They both tore downstairs to find Amy's mother. It is nice to be with a mother in the hail.

CHAPTER FIVE

Little Witch Girl's Birthday Party

One day, Old Witch was very busy up on the bare and bleak glass hill, preparing for her little witch girl's birthday party. It was to be a surprise party, and the first one that the little witch girl had ever had in her life, however long or short that may have been. Amy said she stayed six years old all the time, so it is hard to tell the total.

Amy was talking to Clarissa about Little Witch Girl's birthday right now as she and Clarissa sat drawing at the little table. "You know," Amy said, "that the little witch girl stays six all the time, don't you?"

"Stays six!" shouted Clarissa, who was still a little deaf from her cold. "If she stays six all the time, doesn't she ever have a birthday?"

"What are you shouting for?" asked Amy. Amy was over her cold and was not deaf any more, and had not known that she had ever been a little deaf anyway. "Of course, she has birthdays. You have birthdays whether you stay six or not, don't you?"

"What did you say?" asked Clarissa.

"What's the matter? You deaf or something? I said, of course you have birthdays whether you stay six or not."

"Oh, of course. I forgot. When is her birthday?"

"When? Today. Today is her sixth birthday."

"I thought she was six already. Why won't she be seven? First comes six. And then comes seven."

"Because she stays six, that's why. She stays six years old all the time. Like her cat. He stays six weeks old all the time (I wish ours would) and like Patricia, who stays two." (Patricia was Amy's doll that she put to bed every night and took everywhere with her, her best-beloved doll.) "Patricia came two and she stays two."

"Stays two?" asked Clarissa, cocking her head. "I thought you said, stays six."

"The witch girl stays six!" shouted Amy. "Do you hear me?"

"Yes, stays six. Thought you said, stays two. It's her birthday, but she stays six. That's fair."

"Yes," said Amy. "Stays six always."

"If it's her birthday today, and she stays six—same old thing—doesn't she ever have a birthday party?"

"Yes. She is having a party. Today."

"I wish we could go," said Clarissa, who loved parties, especially the ice cream and the cake.

"Well," said Amy, who was not fond of parties and did not like blowouts, loud singing of "Happy Birthday to You," clapping, or squealing, "we're not witches," she said. "So, we can't go." Amy went on coloring her picture of a witch birthday party. After a thoughtful pause, she said, "I don't think we can. I'm not sure . . ."

"I suppose they can't have any cake at that party," said Clarissa.

"Oh, yes, Old Witch makes it out of herbs. That's what she's probably doing right now, making herb cake."

Amy was right. That was what Old Witch was doing

right then. She prepared herb cake, with herb candles on it, herb-ade (on the order of lime punch) to drink, and rosemary (an herb) ice cream. Next she decorated the witch house with charms, rabbits' feet, miniature black cats (not real ones), baby lizards (real ones), weeny hoppy toads (real ones), and tiny broomsticks. Little witch girls love these things very much—the more the merrier. They squeal with as much delight over hoppy toads and lizards as real little girls do over balloons and lollipops. Then, employing an unusual and complicated abracadabra, Old Witch made everything completely invisible.

Old Witch had invited all the little witches of the witch school. The party was to begin at four o'clock, right after school. While waiting for the little witches to come home, Old Witch spent her time, as she always did lately when she had the chance, looking for the bumblebee and for the lost rune, and wracking her brains to recall how that rune had gone. She sang, as she looked, a little tune that she had made up:

> "In betwixt and in between
> Now, today, and Halloween
> The bee must go for once and all
> E'er one more bite doth me befall."

Meanwhile, at school, a great deal of twittering was going on among the little witch girls. They were making an effort to keep the party a surprise for Little Witch Girl, but their secret whisperings made Little Witch Girl wonder whether stomping and tweaking were going to begin all over again. "Thank goodness for Malachi!" she thought. She had not guessed that this was her birthday, and the little witches, filled with joyous anticipation at being invited to the house of exile of the famous Head Witch, did not give her a clue as to the reason for their high spirits.

So, when school was over, the little witch girl, thinking that this was a day as any other, followed the cardinal home. Had she looked back, she would have been very surprised to see the flock of little witches flying not far behind, but Little Witch Girl did not think to do so.

Old Witch, still humming "In betwixt and in between" greeted her hurriedly. "Come, my dearie dear," she said. "Put on your best dress."

"Why?" asked Little Witch Girl.

"You'll see," said Old Witch.

"No," said Little Witch Girl. "It's play time."

"I'll grantify a wish for you," wheedled Old Witch. "Grantify" is a word Amy made up. It means "grant" and "gratify" at once.

Little Witch thought for a moment before answering. Then her face brightened up. "Oh yes, all right," she said.

So, Little Witch Girl put on her pretty best soft black witch dress. Then she said. "You know what I wish?"

"What?" said Old Witch, croaking fondly and softly. "I'll grantify whatever wish you wish," she said rashly.

"Well, my wish is—now, remember, you promised—for those two real girls, Amy and Clarissa, to come and play with me. Because I'm lonesome. And because I like them."

"Tcluck! Tcluck!" Old Witch groaned. A real witch wish—a witch wish for a million hoppy toads, perhaps—was what she had expected a little witch girl to wish. A witch can never have enough hoppy toads. "Oh, to glory be!" she said. "They banquished me, they did." Then she said firmly, "No! Anything but that!"

"You said *anything*," said the little witch girl. "You can't break your promise."

"I can," said Old Witch. "And I am," she said. "I'm bee-reaking," said Old Witch growing slightly confused (she meant 'breaking'), "my promise right now."

At this moment, fortunately for Old Witch, who was thus saved another bee bite, the clock struck four. Party time! Wind sprang up and wailed. Thunder rumbled. Hailstones bounced against the glass hill. These are the exciting weather conditions under which witch parties always begin. "In thunder, lightning, and in rain!" Old Witch had read these words in a book once, and she knew that they were true.

Sure enough, at this moment, all the little witches swept up. "Surprise!" they squealed. "Surprise!"

Little Witch Girl was speechless with delight. She was truly surprised, and she forgot, for a moment, her wish. What a swishing about of little witch girls on broomsticks! "Happy birthday to you, Happy birthday to you!" they sang. (Some witches, especially those Amy knows about, do sing the same songs as we.)

Old Witch then uttered a famous rune. The little witches, hearing the Head Witch's expert, expressive enunciation, drew back in awe. When the rune was finished, the gifts and the party table all became visible. It was a pretty sight. The little witches made a dive for the hoppy toads to cast warts on themselves and to cast them off again. Old Witch thought that the little witch girl had forgotten all about her wish.

But Little Witch Girl had not forgotten her wish. "Gammer," she said. "Remember your promise. I said I wished Amy and Clarissa could come up here. It's even better now. They can come to the party."

"No," said Old Witch with a horrid croak. "Any wish but that."

"You are breaking your promise," rebuked the little witch girl, and she sat down on the porch in her little red rocker and would not fly with the others. Then, suddenly, the little witch girl remembered an important rule concerning little witches' birthday parties when they occur on the fourth day of the fourth month, and at four o'clock. The rule is that at exactly four minutes past four on that important day, any abracadabra at all will work for the little birthday witch girl.

All fours. Fourth day, fourth month, fourth hour, and fourth minute past four—the combination was magic.

Little Witch Girl rushed into the house. She hopped onto her copy stool, and, just as the hand of the great owlie clock that stood in the cobweb corner reached four minutes past four, it said, "Whoo-whoo, whoo-whoo, whoo-whoo, whoo-whoo," four times, showing how magical a moment this was. It usually whoo-whooed only on the hour and the half-hour.

A hush fell over the group as the little witch girl solemnly chanted the following abracadabra:

"Abracadabra
Cadabra
Cadee
Flying through the air to me

Those two girls from down below
Those two girls—ho-ho, you know."

The wind wailed more loudly than it had four minutes
ago upon the arrival of the little witches. Hail fell again,
and again the thunder boomed. Suddenly these phenomena
ceased. The violet vapors that had accompanied the great
blow cleared. And there, sitting in the middle of the room
at their little yellow table, were the two ordinary real girls,
Amy and Clarissa! The brave banquishers! They were just
sitting at their little yellow table, drawing and coloring
pictures.

The little witch girls stood back and watched them in
silence. To all appearances, Amy and Clarissa thought they
were still at home on Garden Lane, in the big bedroom
behind the high and lofty ginkgo tree.

This was not a true impression. Presently Amy, without looking up from her drawing and speaking in a very
low voice, said to Clarissa, "We are in a haunched house."

Clarissa knew that the word for "haunted" is
"haunched," for Amy had taught it to her.

"Haunched!" she said in her high little voice.

"Yes, sh-sh-sh! Haunched," said Amy.

CHAPTER SIX

In a "Haunched" House

Little Witch Girl looked at Amy and Clarissa in wonder and delight. She had not known that her abracadabra could be that powerful! Old Witch, not knowing either that the rune of a child witch could be that powerful, was waving her hands over a big black pot, paying no attention, interested only in perfecting her brew. Amy, not taking her eyes from her paper, gripped her pencil so hard that her knuckles grew white. Finally, she dared to peek at Old Witch from the corner of her eye. Then, without raising her head, she said to Clarissa, "We be invisible to Old Witch. But remember," she cautioned Clarissa, "not to speak out loud, not to shout, for the house *be* haunched!"

Recovering from their astonishment, all the little witches fluttered around Amy and Clarissa. They felt Amy's light blue dress and Clarissa's pink one. They had never seen pink or blue dresses before, only witch black ones. Even witch party dresses have to be black!

Gradually, Amy and Clarissa grew accustomed to being in this "haunched" witch house, and they did not mind being here, since Old Witch could not see them. Having Old Witch look right through them with her beady eyes made them feel odd, but they grew accustomed to this,

also. Once, to test her invisibility, Clarissa stuck out her
tongue at Old Witch. Old Witch did nothing, which
proved without the shadow of a doubt that she could not
see Clarissa or Amy.

"I never heard of being invisible to one person and not
to the rest," whispered Clarissa, though she saw that, in
this situation, nothing could be more ideal.

Amy told Clarissa that, invisible or not, she must not
stick her tongue out at Old Witch, or any of the witches.
It was not polite. Clarissa saw little sense in this. Why be
invisible and not take advantage of the situation and stick
out your tongue at mean people? However, she obeyed,
and chewed her bubble gum harder instead.

Now the party games were going to begin. The first
game was to be a race on broomsticks around the top of the

glass hill. Old Witch was going to stand at the edge of the hill and hold out her broomstick to the flying witches. On her broomstick she was going to have a great many glass rings and one real gold ring. As they flew past, the little witches must reach for one of these rings. Naturally each witch longed to be the one to get the gold ring and be the winner.

Feeling safe and invisible from Old Witch, Amy and Clarissa longed to take part in this game. Little Witch Girl wanted her guests to play, and urged them to try to ride the broomsticks. But Amy and Clarissa could not make them go. Then Little Witch Girl remembered about two mechanical toy broomsticks that an inventor witch had once given her. One was red and one was blue. These did not work for little witches, but they might work for real little girls. They did! They worked perfectly for Amy and Clarissa, two real, regular little girls, who were used to modern times and mechanical toys and who were not in the least medieval.

First—to practice—Amy and Clarissa flew around the room. Old Witch could not see Amy and Clarissa, but she could see the mechanical broomsticks, all wound up and flying with, seemingly, no one on them. "Get those toys out of here," she said with a croak, "while I'm cooking!" She also took a swat at them as they went past her, so Amy and Clarissa flew their broomsticks outdoors. They were followed by the seven little witches, who shouted, "Head Witch! Head Witch! Come out. We want to race."

So, Old Witch stopped stirring the brew and came out to conduct the gold ring game. She was quite surprised to see the two riderless (to her) broomsticks flying around the top of the hill with the real broomsticks that had each their little witch rider. And she was still more surprised when the red one (Amy's) won. This red mechanical broomstick looked odd flying around the hill top with the gold ring going along beside it like a little planet. Amy was quite used to this game of reaching for the gold ring, for she had seen it played at the merry-go-round in the amusement park above the Potomac. There, however, she was not allowed to reach for the gold ring, lest she fall off her flying horse. Here, she could reach as much as she liked, and—see what had happened! She had been the lucky one to get the gold ring and win the game.

Old Witch glowered suspiciously. She had a deep mistrust of new-fangled mechanical things and relied entirely on ancient runes to make things go, for runes do not break down . . .

"IF THEY BE NOT FORGOTTEN!" hummed a voice gravely in Old Witch's ear.

Old Witch bit her tongue in vexation. If only she could find that lost Malachi rune!

Clarissa had not liked the game on the broomsticks. She didn't like merry-go-rounds or riding ponies. No wonder she did not like broomsticks. And neither she nor Amy liked the careful scrutiny that Old Witch was paying their mechanical broomsticks. Surely Old Witch could see them? Clarissa dared to stick out her tongue again, testing. Nothing happened.

Instead, Old Witch said that it was time for the eating part of the party to commence. They all went into the house, and Old Witch chanted an abracadabra that was so powerful the house shook. The invisible rare herb food came into view! Unfortunately, the invisible real little girls also came into view for Old Witch as well as for the others!

"Oh, to glory be!" gasped Old Witch.

Amy and Clarissa shook in their shoes. They could see that they were no longer invisible to Old Witch, for now her beady eyes were fixed *on* them, not *through* them. "Oh dear," thought Amy. "Now is the time for poison apples or for being baked in the oven!"

"They've been here all along," sang the little witches merrily. "And you didn't know it!" The little witch girls did not realize that Amy and Clarissa were the cause of Old Witch's banishment or they would have been careful not to tease.

"Did too," muttered Old Witch. Then she became very angry. She did not like the idea of having appeared stupid in front of the little witch girls who, no doubt, would tell their teacher. "If you and your partner have come up here playing 'I spy,'" she said to Amy, "you'll find I've been good. Not a rabbit, not a nothing. I haven't been off this hill. You can't revoke Halloween . . . my little rabbits!"

Amy did not like the way that Old Witch said "little rabbits." It sounded like stew for the brew. Once Amy had been to Williamsburg, and there she had had Brunswick stew, which is made with rabbits. "I be not a rabbit," she said. This was the first time that Amy had ever spoken directly to Old Witch, and she thought that she should speak in this special way.

"That may be," said Old Witch. "But there be ways of changing you into one."

Little Witch Girl did not like these words of Old Witch. "Gammer," she said, "you did not mind Amy and Clarissa being here when they were invisible. Why should you mind now that they are in sight? You know you must not be rude."

"BE NOT RUDE!" echoed an emphatic voice.

"Malachi!" Amy whispered in Clarissa's ear. "Be not afraid."

"I be not," said Clarissa who was really frozen with fear.

At the sound of the spelling bee, Old Witch, making a great effort, put some softness into her voice. "Come then, my dears, eat," she said.

While visiting in the witch house, Amy's appetite was not very good. But Clarissa, who had been taken in by the Old Witch's change of manner, had a good appetite regardless of the type of house she was in. Being called "my little rabbit" did not bother her. She had never been to Williamsburg to have Brunswick stew, and she did not get the connection between rabbit and that famous stew. She started to eat her herb ice cream right away, and the little witch girls did too.

But Amy did not eat one bite of anything. She had not forgotten the poison apple in "Snow White" and the gingerbread house in "Hansel and Gretel." She knew far more about witches and their wicked ways than Clarissa did, for she had thought up not only this witch house and the family in it, but the glass hill as well. She was not going to eat one thing!

"Where be the sense," Amy asked herself, "of learning in stories about the wicked ways of witches and then doing the same old thing, eating their good-looking food? And getting in trouble?" She kept her eyes on her friend, Clarissa, who was taking tiny bites of her herb ice cream. Clarissa, thank goodness, did not turn into anything, nor did she fall into a deep one-hundred-year sleep. Not so far. The food smelled good—all the more dangerous.

Smelling it, Amy whispered to Clarissa, "That smells like licker-itch."

Clarissa nodded. "Mm-m," she agreed.

"Or like anise?" suggested Amy.

"Never heard of that," said Clarissa.

"I have it for stomach-ache," said Amy.

Next came the herb cake and the six candles, and it was time for the wish. Little Witch Girl blew out all the candles in one puff so her wish was bound to come true. She would not tell, though urged, what it was. And then she opened her presents, which were of the usual witch variety, toy black cats, cauldrons, broomsticks, and bats. From Old Witch, however, she got a copy of "Old Witch's Famous Big Booke of Runes and Incantations." In it, she had inscribed, "To Hannah, with best wishes, Old Witch." This is the way true authors, witch or otherwise, sign books. Old Witch also gave the little witch girl some new crayons and a small sketch pad.

"What present did you bring?" asked Olie, the rude witch girl, accusingly pointing to the two real girls.

Amy and Clarissa said they were sorry they had not brought a present because they had come unexpectedly. Little Witch Girl politely said that their just being here was present enough for her. However, she would like a remembrance. Could she have Clarissa's bubble gum that Clarissa had stuck to her plate?

"Oh yes," said Clarissa, unsticking it and handing it to Little Witch Girl. "Keep it. You do not have to give it back."

Little Witch Girl was delighted and popped it in her

mouth right away. Being a witch, she could not catch any germs. What a bubble she blew! Being a witch probably had something to do with the size of her bubble. It grew and grew and grew like a huge balloon until it got stuck on the peak of one of the witch hats and popped. While Little Witch Girl was gathering all of this popped bubble gum back into her mouth, Amy felt in her pocket and found a tiny little doll she sometimes kept there.

"Here," she said to the little witch girl. "Would you like this doll? Her name is Little Lydia, and my mother got it for me by abracadabra," she said.

"I didn't know your mother was a witch," said Little Witch Girl.

"A kind of witch," said Amy. "But she needs a scarf to make her abracadabra work. And I know you don't."

"Thank you for the doll," said the little witch girl.

Then Old Witch gathered all the girls, real ones and witch ones, sat them on copy stools before the fireplace, and told stories about her great witch past. How delightedly the little witch girls listened! And how Amy and Clarissa shuddered over her wicked deeds! "One night, I . . ." they all began. And they all ended with, "And that was the end of him, heh-heh!" or, "That was the end of her!"

"My!" thought Amy. "It's a good thing I banquished this mean old wicked old witch up here." The stories that Old Witch told about herself were even worse than the ones Amy's mother told about her.

"Do a wickedness now," implored Olie.

"Yes, yes, yes," beseeched the others, almost tipping over their copy stools.

There was a tense pause. Amy held her breath. Suppose

Old Witch got the idea to take a bite out of her or Clarissa?
Then Old Witch said in great disgust, "Oh, to glory be!
Not a wickedness! Not a hurly-burly!" (A slight buzzing
sound that had been heard in the tense pause subsided.)
"What a dull life for a head witch! No. To do a wicked-
ness, I have to wait for Halloween," she said sarcastically
and hatefully. (The buzzing grew a little louder again.)
"That's what *her* bespake when her bebanquished me!" Old
Witch pointed an awful, accusing, nobby finger at Amy,
and she glowered.

Amy gripped her stool tightly, and she shuddered.

All the little witch girls, except Hannah, frowned at
Amy. They wanted to see a wickedness cast by this real
right famous old witch now and not wait for Halloween.
"Oh, let her," they implored Amy.

They scared Amy as much as Old Witch did, but she
shook her head. "No," she whispered. "She has to be good,"
she said.

The little witch girls fluttered angrily around Amy and
Clarissa. Then Old Witch decided, "The dickens with Halloween!" She would do a wickedness and give the little
witch girls a real party treat that they would never forget. Neither she nor the little witch guests cared about the
warning buzzes, which had become so loud they sounded
like bees in a swarm. Old Witch decided the wickedness
would involve her banquishers.

"I BE . . ." spelled the voice. But what it was going to
say the witches did not know or care. They jeered so
loudly that they drowned it out and would not listen.

"Head Witch be more important than you be, whoever
you be," screamed the little witches. "And anyway who-

ever heard of I B? It's A B! This speller doesn't know its
alphabet. Heh-heh-heh!"

Amy gasped. "You should never make fun of a bumblebee," she whispered to Clarissa.

Little Witch Girl hopped onto the party table. "Stop!"
she ordered. She gave a stirring speech. "Leave these girls
alone!" she said. "You want to have Halloween, don't you?
Go here, go there in front of the Halloween moon, don't
you? Well, you won't be able to if Old Witch casts a wickedness. That is what Amy said!"

There was a moment's silence.

"H E E D!" said the buzzing voice.

But Old Witch heeded only the eager faces of her small
witch admirers. To satisfy her vanity and maintain her
reputation, she decided to cast an awful wickedness and
prove that she was still real, right, mean, old wicked Old
Witch.

At this decision the glass hill shook as though with an
earthquake. (Later Little Witch Girl did find a crack.)
Then Old Witch brushed her own little witch girl off the
party table, got up on it herself, and started the "backanally" dance that always preceded a real wickedness.

At this moment, Little Witch Girl performed a small but
swift backanally herself and said:

> "Malachi!
> Oh, Malachi!
> Malachi, the bumble bye!
> Malachee!
> Oh, Malachee!
> Mumble, bumble
> here to me!"

"Ouch! Ouch! ouch!" screeched all the little witches when this rune had been recited. And, "Ouch!" said Old Witch likewise. They all seemed to be being bitten by a hundred bumblebees. Yet there was but one bumblebee, Malachi, previous tenant of Amy's back yard, rubbed by magic by Old Witch herself, all unbeknownst to her.

Old Witch got so many bites that she had to jump into the cauldron, which, fortunately for her, had cooled. There she soothed her bites with herb soup. All the little witch girls said no more about casting a wickedness. Licking their bites, they mounted their broomsticks and flew away home. Each little witch held onto the broomstick of the one in front. Thus they made a long broomstick train, which was very pretty to see in the gloaming.

It is too bad the party had to end this way, with no door prizes. But witch parties are bound to end just the opposite of ours—in a hurly-burly.

"Good-by, good-by!" Little Witch Girl and Amy and Clarissa yelled after them.

Amy caught a glimpse of Malachi in his camouflage place. He was golden in the last glow of the sun. His three round eyes shone ruby red, and they were alert and anxious. He looked to be frowning. "Thank you, dear Malachi," whispered Amy. "You are a good representatiff."

Malachi spelled quietly, "I DO MY BEST."

Amy and Clarissa went inside. Old Witch, still in the brewing pot, glowered at them. Amy and Clarissa decided they had had enough party and they wanted to go home. They didn't know the way, however. Since they did not know how they had got here, naturally they did not know the way to get back. They were sorry to have caused such a hurly-burly, but after all they had not asked to come.

They sat down at the little yellow table. Thank goodness, their drawings had not been hurt.

"It's been a nice party," said Amy politely to Little Witch Girl.

"Yes," chimed in Clarissa. "Very nice."

"My mother said, be home at six," said Amy.

"Mine too," said Clarissa. "If not before. Because we are having long noodoos for dinner, and they do not wait."

Little Witch Girl gave a sigh. She would have loved to keep these two girls up here and have them for friends always. But of course she knew she couldn't. Who could tell when Old Witch might or might not cast a wickedness? So Little Witch Girl chanted the last half of her four minutes past four birthday abracadabra.

> "Abra
> Cadabra
> Cadee
> Caden.
> Flying through the air
> Again.
> Flying to their homes
> Again.
> Those two girls from down below.
> Twenty and twenty is
> TEN you know."

After this strange rune there came the wailing of wind, the pelting of hailstones, and the violet vapors. When all had cleared, there wasn't a sign of Amy and Clarissa at their little yellow table anywhere on the bare and bleak glass hill. Why should there be? They were right at home in Amy's mother's room, high up behind the ginkgo tree, still coloring pictures—of witches.

"Abra, cadabra, cadee, caden," chanted Amy happily and busily.

It sounded rather merry the way she sang this little tune, and no hailstones appeared at all. No wind, either.

"Good-by," said Clarissa. "I have to go home now."

"Good-by, good-by, cadee, cadum," sang Amy, busily making buzzes on her drawing and singing, "Oh Malachi, the bumblebye, the bumblebye, the bumblebee . . ."

CHAPTER SEVEN

The Mermaid Lagoon

The next day Amy and Clarissa were swinging together in the little back yard. Together they went up and together they came down, over and over exactly together. Because of this harmonious way of swinging, they could carry on a conversation. They were talking about Little Witch Girl.

"Ts," said Amy tenderly. "It must be very lonesome up there for Little Witch Girl with no one around except Old Witch and the little school witches, who all look exactly alike. No sisters. No brothers. Nothing."

"Up where?" asked Clarissa.

"Where! On the bare, bleak glass hill! You know! You were there yesterday. You ought to know! You might not be here today if it were not for Malachi. He saved your life, remember!"

"Oh yes, of course," said Clarissa, trying hard to remember. She had a hard time remembering what happened this morning, let alone yesterday!

"Well," Amy went on. "I think she is lonesome. Don't you think so, Clarissa?"

"Yes," said Clarissa.

"And," said Amy, "even though Old Witch can be very nice—sometimes she is very nice, isn't she, Clarissa? She was nice not to eat us, wasn't she? She didn't even eat one finger. And that wouldn't have been so bad, you know, if she had eaten one finger because we would still have nine. Still, she is too old for Little Witch Girl to play with every minute. That's what I mean."

"Yes," agreed Clarissa. "Very antique." Clarissa knew several hard words, having been born in Paris, France.

"Antique, but good," said Amy. "She is good right now (Malachi is keeping her good), and she better stay good, or she knows what will happen to her—no Halloweeny!"

For a moment the conversation stopped. They swung in silence. Halloween was a long way off. Spring, instead, was in the air in Washington, though not, of course, on the bare and bleak glass hill. There, since nothing could grow, as Amy had decreed in her banishment orders, the hill, in all seasons, remained glass, plain, bare, slippery glass. There, the only way that you could tell spring was in the air was to look at the sky, the soft and gracious blue spring sky. But most witches do not do this. Usually they just look at the ground for toads and do not know whether there is a spring sky or not. Naturally they prefer storm and hail and wind and rain to anything that could be called soft and gracious. The wilder the weather, the more gleefully they say, "Heh-heh."

Not so with Little Witch Girl. She went around with her head way back, not to miss a minute of soft spring sky. "Hurrah! Hurrah!" she shouted, holding out her arms wide to grab all the beauty to her.

And not so, either, with old Malachi, the bumblebee. His musty dry fuzzy coat was taking on new sheen and gloss, and he looked as soft as golden plush. He had to push more deeply into his camouflage place in order to avoid the searching beady eyes of Old Witch.

But down here in Washington, where Amy and Clarissa were swinging, everything was as fresh as spring could make it. In the parks and in the gardens, early flowers were blooming—forsythia, crocuses, and snowdrops. Trees were beginning to bud, the birds said, "Twee-eet, twee-eet," and everything was beautiful.

"Ts," said Amy, shaking her head pensively. "And no flowers can grow up there either."

"No flowers?" asked Clarissa, beginning to feel sad, too. Clarissa was rarely sad. A happier little girl could hardly be found. But, no flowers! "Not even Indian pipe?" she asked, trying to think up the least pretty flower that she could.

"None," said Amy. "None. Just plain N O N E," she said. Amy was a happy little girl, too. But she enjoyed being sad sometimes, especially when she had been the one to think up the sadness.

"Poor little witch girl," said Clarissa.

And the two swung back and forth, back and forth.

After a while they jumped off the swing. Then they went indoors, this lovely spring day, and started to draw pictures. Amy drew a waterfall for Little Witch Girl, with a little mermaid behind it, she felt that sorry for her. "Here is a nice sort of friend," she thought. "I would like to have a mermaid for a friend myself."

Now, up there on the bare glass hill, Little Witch Girl was not having too bad a time after all. Old Witch, to make up for her would-be wickedness at the birthday party yesterday, had tied a heavy rope to the one strong pole left on the rickety porch. In the end of the rope she had tied a bulky knot that Little Witch Girl could sit on. Then, holding tightly to the rope with both legs, Little Witch Girl could take off from the porch, sail over the edge of the glass hill, and then hoist herself back up. This one-rope swing was on the order of one tied to Polly Knapp's linden tree.

Tired of watching the sky, Little Witch Girl was swinging now. She could sail off in practically any direction, and she was exploring the hill, as far down as she could reach with her toes, feeling for cracks and crannies. Yesterday's hurly-burly had created a number of cracks that had not been there before. Little Witch Girl had her shoes off so that she could dig her toenails, that were like little bird's claws, into the glass hill. She enjoyed scraping them over the smooth glass.

Suddenly, what did her toes come upon but a hole in the hill! She found that it was big enough for both feet to get into at the same time. In fact, she found that it was big enough for a thin little witch girl to get her whole self into, and this she did. Leaving the rope dangling on the outside, where it would be handy for the return trip, but taking her broomstick with her, tied to her waist like a sword, she went inside the bare and bleak glass hill, exploring.

What an enchanting path stretched ahead of her! It wound invitingly into the middle of the clear glass hill. Beautiful colors, such as sparkle in a prism, or a diamond, a drop of water, or a tear, dazzled her. Breathless at this shimmering beauty, Little Witch Girl tiptoed slowly down the path. Tinkling sounds could be heard, faintly and far-away, like fairy music.

"My!" said Little Witch Girl. "It is like being inside a soap bubble."

Then she came upon the most enchanting sight of all, a small waterfall! Real water was dropping from one glass ledge to another. And peeking out at Little Witch Girl from behind the waterfall, there was a radiant little mermaid. She seemed to be of exactly the same size and age as Little Witch Girl, and that was, you know, the same as Amy and Clarissa. The little mermaid had also long blond hair. But right now hers was very wet. She was shaking it dry in the golden reflection of the noontime sun, way way way on the outside.

"Hello," she said politely, looking at the little witch girl in surprise. "Who are you?"

"Hannah," said Little Witch Girl shyly. "Who are you?"

"Lurie," said the little mermaid. "Will you play with me?" She spoke crooningly, and her voice had a lovely sort of sigh in it, like the hush, hush of gentle waves on rocks, so that it would have been quite impossible not to play with her. But, of course, Little Witch Girl wanted very much to play with her, and happily nodded yes. The little mermaid reminded Little Witch Girl of Amy, not the bottom fish part, but the top blond-headed part.

"Oh, we must first give the baby her bottle," said the little mermaid. "I almost forgot."

("You know," said Amy to Clarissa, beginning to draw a mermaid baby, "that a baby sister was what the little witch girl wished for for herself at her party, don't you?" "No, I didn't know that," said Clarissa. "Now you know," said Amy. "When she sees this mermaid baby, she'll wish for one more than ever.")

"Baby! Bottle!" exclaimed the little witch girl.

"Yes. My baby sister. Named Babay," said the little mermaid.

"Babay!" gasped Little Witch Girl. "O-o-oh! How wonderful! Could I see her? I never heard of a mermaid baby before. Just real big mermaids are all I ever heard about. I never heard of a mermaid girl either, and yet— here you are!"

"Don't they teach you anything in school?" asked Lurie.

"Oh, my yes. We learn about, well . . . toads."

"Ugh," said the little mermaid. "I like frogs, but I do not like ugly toads. I'm glad I don't go to your school."

"Well. Where's Babay?" asked the little witch, who was anxious not to get into an argument about school. Naturally, everybody—real girls, witch girls, and mermaid girls—thinks their school is the best and says, "Rah, rah, rah!" when their school wins.

"She's sleeping now," said the little mermaid. "Under the water lilies. But she may have waked up and she may want her bottle."

The water lilies were not real. They were glass and of many colors. Despite being hard and cold, they were very beautiful. Little Witch Girl peeped under them. "O-o-oh!" she said. An exquisite little mermaid baby lay on a glass lily leaf, fast asleep. She had her tail tucked under her, and her thumb was in her mouth.

The little mermaid decided not to wake her up for her bottle. "It is not good to wake a baby up, you know," she said.

Little Witch Girl did not know this. But she was glad to learn it. Suppose she ever had a witch baby sister? Then she would know not to wake the baby up. "Where do you get the milk?" she asked curiously.

"From our mermaid cow."

"O-o-oh!" said the little witch girl. "And where is she?"

"Down there. If you put your ear to the ground, you will hear a moo, and that is our cow."

Little Witch Girl put her ear to the ground, and she did hear a very faint moo, a rather lonely and plaintive "moo-moo."

"Could I see her?" she asked.

"Oh no, she is too shy," said the little mermaid. "Now," she said. "Let's have a little swim."

"Swim!" exclaimed Little Witch Girl. "We are not allowed to do that. I never even had my hat off until the day I came."

"Well, I feel dry and brittle," said the little mermaid.

"Come on in the water. You can swim with your hat on."

"I don't know how to swim," admitted the little witch girl, ashamed.

"Don't know how to swim! What can you do?" asked the little mermaid.

"Fly," said Little Witch Girl. "Of course, on my broomstick."

"Well. I can't do that," said the mermaid. "But I can flip over the waterfall, and that is almost like flying." And she swam across the lagoon and flipped herself down and over the waterfall.

"Fine," said Little Witch Girl. "That was pretty. Now. How do you get back?"

"I have to swim up the waterfall, and, believe me, that is hard. It sometimes takes me a whole day." She lay on a glass rock and leaned on her elbow. "But, don't go away," she said crooningly. "Stay."

Little Witch Girl had absolutely no idea of going. "I won't go," she promised. "Perhaps I can get you back more quickly with a rune I just learned called 'From low to high.'"

"Hm-m-m," said the little mermaid thoughtfully, from down below. "You sound like a witch. You even look like one. I just noticed. Are you a witch?"

"Oh my, yes. I'm real, right, regular Little Witch Girl." A slight croak had crept into the little witch's voice.

"Oh, isn't that nice, to be a witch?" said the little mermaid. "But you will not cast a spell on me, will you? You will not change me into all fish, or all person?"

"Oh, no," assured the little witch girl. "I'll just try and get you up over the waterfall."

In her slightly hoarse and charming voice, Little Witch Girl chanted:

"Abracadabra
A B C
Mermaid lass of the glass hill sea,
A-flip your tail
And a-flop to me
Twenty and twenty is ten
you see."

The little mermaid landed with a splash in the lagoon at Little Witch Girl's feet. "My, that's smart!" she said.

Little Witch Girl was proud, but modestly said nothing.

Then, of course, the little mermaid wanted to try to ride the broomstick. But she had no better luck than Amy and Clarissa had had. She could not make it go and kept slipping off it and falling with a splash into the lagoon. The little witch girl had not yet learned the magic that would enable someone else to ride her broomstick without falling off. She was going to study this hard abracadabra soon, probably before Halloween.

"Well," said Little Witch Girl to cheer up the little mermaid. "You can swim. And I can fly. That's fair, isn't it?"

The two little girls then rested a while and had a conversation about their lives. The little mermaid told Little Witch Girl about her school, and Little Witch Girl told Lurie about hers. She also told Lurie about her friends, Amy and Clarissa. And she said, "You shall be my best friend and I shall be yours. Amy and Clarissa are best friends, and we shall be best friends, too."

To seal this friendship, the little mermaid pulled out one

of her prettiest, most iridescent scales and gave it to the little witch girl. She, in turn, gave the little mermaid a tiny glass canoe that she got out of thin air and by way of abracadabra. Then they kissed each other and vowed to remain best friends forever.

Now it was time for the little witch to go home. "I have to go," she said.

The little mermaid shook her head and smiled. "Oh, no, you don't," she crooned, and a lovely lulling note came into her voice. Little Witch Girl felt her eyes closing. She almost fell asleep. Fortunately, she was sitting on her broomstick and a stiff straw stuck into her, reminding her that she was a little witch girl and belonged in the witch family, and that her home was on top of the glass hill and not inside it, however lovely the mermaid lagoon might be. Moreover, she heard a buzzing voice that admonished her sternly, "A W A K E N!" So, rousing herself and promising that she would come often, she mounted her broomstick and flew down the enchanting glass path.

"Good-by, good-by," they called to each other as long as they could hear.

When Little Witch Girl reached the entrance way, there was the heavy rope outside, and she swung herself up and onto the porch, where she sat down in her little red rocker and rocked. She paid no attention to Old Witch who was thumbing again through her big book of runes.

"I thought it was in here," she muttered. She was looking for the loose clipping that had the rune of Malachi, the bumblebee, on it. She thought that if she tore it up, his magic would disappear, and this was probably true. Fortunately, Little Witch Girl did not know what Old

Witch was looking for and did not have to think must she,
or must she not, give it up. So far, the Malachi rune was
safe in the hem of Little Witch Girl's cloak.

Little Witch Girl decided not to tell her gammer Old
Witch about the little mermaid or the mermaid lagoon.
They were her own shining secrets. "My," she thought.
"What a wonderful day! That Babay! She was so cunning!
If only I had a baby sister, too! Then I would have every-
thing," she thought. "The baby could try to put its toe in
its mouth." Sighing, she rocked back and forth, back and
forth . . .

CHAPTER EIGHT

The Baby Witch

One day, Old Witch was poring over all her books, searching for a rune that would get the magic off Malachi—wherever he was—that someone (it was she, but she didn't know it) had magic-ed onto him. She looked under bumble, and bee, and Malachi, and magic, and bites, and stings; also under plain antidotes for magic. "Let's see," she muttered. "What about sewing bees? A sewing bee might sew up a spelling bee." She was so absorbed that she didn't hear the murmur of the bee, "MEND THY WAYS!" Nor did she hear anything Little Witch Girl said. "I might as well not talk," thought Little Witch Girl.

Little Witch Girl sat lonesomely rocking in her little red rocker. There was no one to talk to. She had been to the mermaid lagoon to play with Lurie. But neither Lurie nor Babay had been there. Perhaps they had swum away, way inside, to search for the beginning of the lagoon or to milk the mermaid cow. Little Witch Girl had waited for a while. She loved the many-colored pool. Dipping her fingers in it, she watched the drops falling from her fingers, like miniature soap bubbles. Suddenly she had begun to feel lonesome. "Lurie!" she had called. "Who-whoo!"

Her echo scared her. "Lur-eee . . . whowhoo-oo-oo!" it answered as with a sigh. The echo did not seem to want

to stop. Frightened, Little Witch Girl had flown home as
fast as she could. So, there she was, sitting in her little red
rocker, having a lonesome rock. It is sad to go looking for
your best friend to play with and then for her not to be
there. At this low, lonesome moment who should fly up
but the red cardinal bird, Amy's emissary. He dropped a
tightly folded little wad of paper in Little Witch Girl's lap.
"Twee-eet!" he sang, and then he flew away.

"O-o-oh!" said Little Witch Girl, squealing with joy.
"It's a letter from Amy!"

Is there anything nicer, when you feel lonesome, than to
get a letter from a person whom you love very much?
She could hardly bear to read it, she was so happy. Finally,
she read:

"Dear Little Witch Girl,

Thank you for the birthday party in your house. How
do you like the little mermaid? Fine? But she isn't there
every time when you go and say, 'Can you play?' Well,
it is the same with me and Clarissa. Sometimes she isn't
there either. Sometimes she goes and plays with Polly
Knapp. And that is when I wish most of all that I had a
baby sister. Your birthday wish was for a baby sister,
wasn't it? I thought so. Why not try for one with your
abracadabra, or have Old Witch try?

I love you and you love me,
Amy.

P.S. Mind that Old Witch does not find Malachi, or the
magic rune. BEE seeing you. A."

Old Witch, as well as Malachi, saw the letter in Little
Witch Girl's lap, and she knew at a glance that it was from
Amy.

"What does that banquisher want now?" she demanded irritably.

Little Witch Girl didn't even hear. She read the letter three times more. And then she happily sat, and she rocked, and she thought.

Old Witch peered curiously at Little Witch Girl from the doorway. After a while, she said, "Well, Hannah. What's the news?"

Little Witch Girl stood up. A happy glow was on her face.

"Gammer?" she said.

"Eh?" croaked Old Witch.

"You don't know it, of course. But you know what I wished for on my birthday candles that I blew out in one blow? And if you blow out all the candles in one blow, it means your wish will come true."

"No," said Old Witch.

"Well, I wished for a baby sister. That's what I wished for. And now. Listen to this. Just listen." Little Witch Girl read the letter aloud. When she finished she said, "Oh, gammer! Isn't that wonderful?"

Old Witch was not as pleased. "Baby witch!" she said. "Oh, to glory be!" Old Witch did not want any weeny witch around. Weeny rabbits, fat and juicy, that she could pop into her mouth and eat up were what she wanted. Let Little Witch Girl try and get a baby witch herself with her own abracadabra—heh-heh!—for Old Witch knew that she wouldn't do the getting.

"Just think! A baby sister!" said Little Witch Girl. She could not imagine Old Witch not being as pleased as she was.

"A baby sister, now!" said Old Witch, as though her

mind had not already been made up that she did not want any baby witch around.

"Yes," said Little Witch Girl. "Then I would never be lonesome."

"Well, you don't have one, heh-heh!" Old Witch said with a rasping croak.

"Couldn't you get me one? You're the real, right, regular Head Old Witch. You know the abracadabra, don't you? It says here in this important letter that you do," pleaded Little Witch Girl. "Oh, please, dear old gammer Old Witchie! Please!"

"I could. But I won't. No!" said Old Witch with a terrible croak.

"Well, I'm going to get one myself, you'll see," said Little Witch Girl with a sob. "And right this very minute, too."

So, Little Witch Girl piped this chant. Her voice was pretty and high when she was excited.

> "Abracadabra
> A B C
> Flying through the air to me
> Hotch
> Cotch
> In the Potch
> A weeny witchie baby
> Do I see?"

Apparently this was not the right abracadabra for getting a witch baby. Nothing came flying through the air. Disconsolately, Little Witch Girl sat down on her heels, covered her face with her hands, and sobbed silently.

In spite of herself Old Witch began to feel sorry for the

little witch girl. (She must be getting good, willy-nilly.) And she reasoned in this way. "After all, *I* got *her*—that's Little Witch Girl—with abracadabras when *I* was lonesome. Now, maybe I should get *her* a baby sister, now that *she* is lonesome. I don't know. I don't know," she muttered with a witch sigh, which is on the order of a cold blast of wind.

A loud sob escaped from Little Witch Girl who rarely wept even when she bumped her nose.

This decided Old Witch. "Yes, I suppose I should. And yes, I suppose I shall," she said.

Having made the important decision, Old Witch lost no time in doing something about it. She bent over and got into the position for uttering great abracadabras. Wiggling back and forth and waving her arms about with strange and frightening movements, she chanted this chant:

> "Abracadabra
> Cadabra
> Cadee
> C B A and
> A B C
> Flying through the air to WE
> Fiddly
> Widdly
> Biddly
> BEE
> Here's a weeny witchie just for
> SHE!"

Of course this was a much more powerful abracadabra than Little Witch Girl's had been. To learn to say it properly, Old Witch had probably had to go to the witch and wizard school for centuries. It should, therefore, work. And, it did work!

Flying through the air, strapped to a miniature broomstick, there came a weeny witch baby. She came complete with little witch hat, loose-flowing, soft little black witch clothes, and with a tiny, scrawny black kitten miaowing fiercely and clinging to the broomstick, sometimes right side up, sometimes wrong side up.

"HERE BE BABY," spelled the voice of Malachi. Little Witch Girl took her hands off her tear-streaked face. Awe-stricken, she sat back on her haunches. "O-o-oh!" she gasped as she watched the weeny witch baby come to a neat landing on the little brass bed. "Oh! Isn't she cute!"

Old Witch was surprised herself. "Oh, to glory be!" she muttered. "Who ever would have thought that I could do anything as smart as that? Up on this bare and bleak place of banishment my magic is rusty. Yet see what I did!" She felt quite proud. Witch babies are very rare. Giving an amiable, not an awful, heh-heh, she too sat back on her haunches. It is quite exhausting to do great magic.

"Now," she croaked. "We be quite a family, ben't we? All generations be represented here now."

"THAT BE RIGHT," confirmed a solemn voice. Feeling rather confused, Old Witch studied matters. She wondered if getting this weeny witch out of thin air meant that she was being a good or a bad witch, according to the rules and regulations laid down by Amy, the banquisher. Good or bad? Finally, she decided that, since the suggestion to get Witch Baby had come from Amy, she was being good. At the same time, she was also being a successful witch. Here was one occasion, she decided, when "good" applied both to witch and to Amy rules. "Oh, to glory be!" she said. "Here I be, pleasing everybody."

"We'll have to get her a cradle," said the little witch girl, staring at her little sister in love and admiration. "Oh!" she said. "See its hands, its tiny hands! Did you ever see such hands? I wonder about its feet. Could we see its feet?"

"Tcluck, tcluck, tcluck," said Old Witch, still quite pleased with herself. This clucking sound was like music to Weeny Witch's ears, and the baby flashed a sudden, endearing smile.

"Not right now," said Old Witch. She bent over the little witch baby. "She has to have her bottle now, doesn't she?"

"Cr-cr-cr," crooned the weeny witchie baby.

"O-o-oh!" breathed Little Witch Girl. She gasped with delight over every single thing that the baby did.

Old Witch busied herself right away, preparing the little witch baby's herb formula. And while Old Witch was not looking, the little witch girl could not resist taking a peek at the little witch baby's feet. She turned back the baby's robes, which were as soft as the silkiest black cobwebs, and she saw that the weeny witch's feet were encased in softest, thinnest, most transparent little black booties. Since she had kicked one of them off, Little Witch Girl gently tied it back on. The color of the ribbons was pale pink!

Again Little Witch Girl was astonished. She didn't know that weeny witch babies were allowed to have pink ribbons. She thought black, everything black, plain, regular, real, right witch black. "They must be a present from Amy," Little Witch Girl decided happily.

"She has to have a cradle right away," said the little witch girl again. "Look how she kicks. She might roll off my bed! I'll try to get her the cradle."

So, Little Witch Girl said an abracadabra, but it still did not work, despite the great wiggling around that she had done in imitation of Old Witch. However, she did get a rattle, and Old Witch got the cradle from thin air and by way of abracadabra. In the cradle were soft black blankets and a warm little black bunny suit for cold days. Now the witch baby had everything.

"Abr-abr-abr," she gurgled happily when she was settled in her cradle.

"She is trying to say abracadabra," said Little Witch Girl.

Little Witch Girl and old gammer Old Witch marveled at the brightness of the little one.

"Very bright baby," observed Old Witch with a gentle croak. "What does the serpent say?" she asked the baby.

"Sss, sss," said Baby.

"And what does the hoppy say?" asked Old Witch.

Baby gave a trill like a tree toad.

"What'd I say?" said Old Witch. "Here's a bright one, all right."

Little Witch Girl was so entranced with the baby witch that she could do nothing but stand at the side of the cradle and watch her and watch her and watch her. Long and silently she stood there watching, with one hand on the cradle, gently rocking it. She refused to go to school because all she could do was stay beside the cradle and rock it and stare at the weeny witch and exclaim over her enchanting ways.

"Look at the darling little curled-down nose she has!" she exclaimed.

"Tcluck!" said Old Witch.

"And curled-up chin," added Little Witch Girl.

"Tcluck!" said Old Witch.

"And look," said Little Witch Girl. "She already knows me. She says cr-cr-cr to me whenever she looks at me."

"Trying to croak already, the smart little thing," said Old Witch with a fond heh-heh. This sound was music to Weeny Witchie's ears, and she clapped her hands together, making sparks fly.

"Tcluck!" said Old Witch. Making sparks fly from fingers is a talent limited to only a few witches. "Unusual, she is. Talented. Oh, to glory be!"

For a moment Little Witch Girl was ashamed of her lack of skill, for she could not make sparks fly from her fingers. Some witches happen to be born with this skill. Others are not. Naturally, if you are a witch, it comes in very handy to be able to shake out sparks. Little Witch Girl felt a little jealous of Weeny Witchie. She wished that someone would tell some cute thing that she had done when she was a baby. Then she managed to overcome her twinge of jealousy and awaited the next fireworks, as she called making sparks.

But that was all for now. The little witch baby had fallen asleep. Her deep breathing was the only sound that could be heard in the house of the witch family. Wonderful peace and quiet settled over them all, the sort of quiet that comes when there is a new little baby sleeping in the house.

Little Witch Girl could not take her eyes off Weeny Witchie even while she was sleeping. She got her red rocker and she rocked beside the baby's cradle, singing pretty witch lullabies. "Sleep, witchie, sleep," she sang. "Bye, baby bye," she sang, and other gentle tunes. Now and then, when Weeny Witchie waked up, she asked to hold her and to give her her bottle. This Old Witch graciously permitted. Then she rocked her and sang to her some more. It was the most wonderful day of Little Witch Girl's whole life.

Once she said, "Gammer?"

"Eh?" asked Old Witch who was peacefully reading her runes.

"What shall we name her?" asked Little Witch Girl.

"BEEBEE!" spelled the spelling voice.

"That's a very good name," said Little Witch Girl. And she thought, "It is almost like Babay." Then she added aloud, "Gammer. Malachi should be the baby's godfather, since he named her."

"BYE, BEEBEE, BYE," sang the spelling bee peacefully. "SAIL ACROSS THE SKY."

Old Witch said nothing. She just did not like any reference to Malachi and she did not like the sound of his voice.

Little Witch Girl sometimes told the baby witchie stories about Amy and Clarissa, the banquishers of Old Witch and the befrienders of her. "Cr-cr-cr," the little witch baby would gurgle happily. She liked to hear songs and stories about these two brave girls.

As for Old Witch, she became very fond of Weeny Witchie. The baby seemed to bring out the best in her, and she was quite busy with preparing the formula and other work that had to do with Beebee. She had less time for searching out wicked runes, and Malachi, the bumblebee, Amy's representative, did not have to sting Old Witch for some days.

Unfortunately, however, the little black bunny suit that had come with the witch baby's cradle and which the baby Tommy kitten slept on, kneading it like bread, often reminded Old Witch of rabbits—rabbits to eat. It began to be that she could not get rabbits out of her mind.

So, Malachi became anxious and watchful again, and he kept himself in readiness for what might happen. "BE PREPARED!" seemed to be his motto.

CHAPTER NINE

The Painting Field

Today, Amy and Clarissa were drawing pictures of the Easter Bunny and the eggs he was painting in the painting field. Old Witch happened to be in Amy's picture, too. She was up in the corner, sitting on the glass hill. She had her telescope in her hands and was looking down.

"Some people think," said Amy to Clarissa, "that, with Little Witch Girl and Weeny Witchie living with her, Old Witch never was wicked again."

"Yes," said Clarissa. "Except on Halloween."

"Well, Clarissa. She didn't stay good," said Amy ominously. "Look at her now. She can't forget about the—you know what—the rabbits. She's getting wicked all over again, I think."

Clarissa smiled approvingly. But, pretending despair, she clutched her head between her hands. "Oh, to glory be!" she said, imitating Old Witch. Ever since the witch birthday party, Amy and Clarissa both used a number of Old Witch's expressions, which they had picked up on that famous day. Amy's mother did not like the way Amy said, "Heh-heh!"

"You will ruin your voice," she said.

Both little girls laughed, and saying, "Heh-heh-heh!" they went on coloring.

Meanwhile, up on the glass hill, Old Witch sat rocking on the rickety porch. As she rocked, she peered intently down into the valley below. Her telescope was in her lap. Now and then she seized it excitedly and focused it on the painting field. She liked what she saw. She drooled, licked her chops, and said, "Yum, yum, yum."

"Be good!" she muttered sarcastically. "That's what that banquisher ordered. What I'm doing is, I'm turning into a regular old rocking-chair woman, losing my witch skill." She rocked so hard for a moment that the chair nearly went over backward. Seizing her telescope again, she studied the painting field. "I'm not Head Witch of all the witches for nothing. Am I?

"No!" she croaked. Her croak was so awful that it produced a clap of thunder and a flash of lightning. There was also a loud foreboding buzz to which she paid no heed, nor to the bite she suddenly received. Shouting "Heh-heh!" Old Witch jumped up, cavorted around the porch, did the backanally, and again seized her telescope. This telescope was so strong and magical that if someone winked twenty miles away, Old Witch could see the wink. Again she turned it upon the painting field.

From his camouflage place on the porch Malachi did not need a telescope to see what Old Witch saw. With his two compound telescopic eyes, he could see much farther than people, even witch people, do. Malachi had no difficulty in spotting now what was employing Old Witch's attention.

Hundreds of little rabbits, painting the eggs for Easter in their painting field. That is the scene that Old Witch with her telescope, and Malachi with his telescopic eyes, could see. To Malachi, the sight was a worry and a responsibility. To Old Witch it was a pleasant and enticing one, and she made crunching sounds with her two long teeth. She brushed the air around her head as though ridding it of what sounded like an angry bumblebee, though she could not see it. "That bee be not going to get the better of me!" she muttered with irritation.

Now, as has been said before, rabbits were what this old witch liked best in the whole world to eat. She was also fond of their painted Easter eggs. The more prettily painted they were, the better she liked them, and she ate shell and

all. Yes, and she needed rabbits for purposes other than for plain eating. Their paws she needed for charms to give to captured princes to help them win the pretty princess. In return the prince would have to forfeit his first-born child to her or else be blinded in the brambles. Catching rabbits had been Old Witch's greatest wickedness in the days before Amy had banished her to the bare and bleak glass hill. And Old Witch, watching the rabbits below in the painting field, made up her mind to fly down the glass hill on her broomstick and steal rabbits. She chose not to remind herself that if Amy discovered this wickedness (and how could

Amy help but discover it, since Amy was in charge of all that was going on?), she would have to forfeit the right to be the real Halloween witch who sails across the sky that night.

"On to the painting field!" she screeched. She liked this rallying cry and repeated it again and again.

Old Witch got her powerful old weather-beaten broomstick from behind the door. She rode around the room on it saying, "Heh-heh!" and causing Little Witch Girl and Weeny Witchie to laugh miniature wicked "heh-hehs." Then she uttered the following abracadabra:

> "Abracadabra
> A B C
> What is it that I do see?
> Hotch
> Cotch
> In the Potch
> Rabbits, rabbits
> for wicked ME."

Then she said, "Tcluck-tluck," to her broomstick and she screeched, "Oh, the hurly-burly!" Old Tom leaped on the broomstick, and whee-ee! off they flew.

Though it was early April, a terrible cold wind sprang up. Black clouds darkened the sky, thunder rumbled, and lightning flashed. Down below in the painting field, at these awful manifestations, signs, and portents, the rabbits pricked up their long antennae ears. Their alarm was furthered, their fears confirmed by the arrival of Malachi, the bumblebee, who had shot down from the glass hill like a streak of neon light, preceding Old Witch by minutes only and buzzing loudly as he came.

"WICKED OLD WITCH BE ON THE WAY. THUS
SHE DISOBEYS THE RULES OF AMY! SHE
COMES! MY BITES SHE HEEDS NOT! MY WARN-
INGS SHE HEEDS NOT! I PROPHESY YOUR EX-
TINCTION IF YOU DO NOT ACT SWIFTLY. TO
YOUR POSTS, RABBITS. I WILL TO MINE. I MUST
NOT LONG LEAVE LITTLE WITCH GIRL OR
WEENY WITCH."

Since Malachi spelled all these words as he frenziedly
darted here and there, and since this was a much longer
speech than he ordinarily gave, the rabbits recognized their
dire need for action. Buzzing a final portentous warning
in Headman Rabbit's ear, "RABBITS, BEWARE!" Malachi flew back, a long streak of golden light against the
blackened sky, to his camouflage place on the witch's porch.

Rabbits are very clever animals. They knew that Old
Witch was their worst enemy. They knew how much she
liked to catch rabbits and pop them into her old black
shawl, to make into a stew, if not to eat them whole as they
were! And also, they knew she liked to make use of them
in abracadabras and incantations, all of which were horrible for rabbits. Rabbits are not interested in being charms
for princes, however much in danger the princes may be.
Nor do they like to have one of their paws hanging from
someone's key ring. They like to lead their own life, whatever it may be. In this case it was painting Easter eggs.

Not long ago, Head Easter Rabbit had had a message
from Amy saying that Old Witch was good now and that
the rabbits need not worry about her except, possibly, on
Halloween. Halloween was the only time that Old Witch
was going to be allowed to be the wicked old witch, and
Amy advised all rabbits to hide then, just plain hide. Still,

Head Rabbit worried anyway. He rightfully knew Old Witch too well to take any chances, and he had warned all rabbits to be on guard against her at all times. Even while the rabbits were painting their eggs, he had guards stationed all over the painting field in case Old Witch should return. He often held witch drills, just as you have fire drills, and every single rabbit—man, mother, and child—knew what he or she was expected to do in case of witch emergency.

So now, at Malachi's terrifying predictions, Head Rabbit sounded the witch alarm. He blew the trumpet. He clanged the cymbals, and every single rabbit ran to his post and did what he had been rehearsed to do.

First they rolled their painted eggs (the child rabbits helped with this job) into a great and vaulted cave. Mothers and small rabbit children stayed there. Then, from out of the cave, the rabbits rolled hundreds of round rocks, which they had long ago, in the slack season, painted to look exactly like Easter eggs in case Old Witch should return and with which they hoped to deceive her.

Then they got out all the Easter bunnies, the toy ones stuffed with sawdust and cotton, which they were going to deliver to Amy and Clarissa and other boys and girls on Easter eve. They stood these toy rabbits here and there all over the painting field and placed wet brushes in their paws. Beside each of the toy rabbits, which they hoped would be taken for real ones, they placed piles of the pretty painted rocks, which they hoped would be taken for the real painted Easter eggs.

They finished these artful preparations just in the nick of time, for the awful "heh-heh" of the wicked old witch could now plainly be heard. Every single rabbit then, with the exception of one, Brave Jack by name, who was to be the signal corps all by himself, dived into the cave.

This cave was situated in the middle of the painting field. It had once been a cyclone cellar belonging to a lovely old mansion, which had burned down years ago. It was hidden by high bushes, so it was unknown to man and beast, except for the rabbits and their good friends, the titmice, and other little field animals. Even Old Witch knew nothing about this cave. She could not get into it with abracadabra because she did not know about it. You cannot ask to get into something with magic if you do not know that it exists.

"Heh-heh!" she cackled as she idled her broomstick high over the silent field. Her greedy eyes could now, without the help of her telescope, take in the tempting sight of all the little rabbits (toy ones) stationed all around with piles of painted eggs (rocks) beside them.

If only Old Witch would gather up the toy rabbits and rock eggs in her greed and never know the difference!

CHAPTER TEN

Danger in the Painting Field

It was as still as night in the painting field. Brave Jack was in position, alerted to give the rabbits in their hideout news, warnings, and general information concerning Old Witch.

"Who will be the guard?" Head Rabbit had asked.

"I will," Brave Jack had quickly answered—to everyone's relief. Rabbits are very timid, and none of them would *like* the job of staying outside in the danger, instead of inside in a nice safe cyclone cellar that—they hoped—Old Witch knew nothing about. Brave Jack was as timid as all the rest. But someone had to say, "I will," and he had been the one to say it. This shows that he had a special sort of bravery way inside upon which he could count, timid or not, in any sort of rough pinch such as this, the coming of great Old Witch. So, he took up his post beside a small, secret passageway, hidden by a pot of green paint, that led into the main one to the cyclone cellar. If need be, and if he had time to do so, he could escape this way.

The plot was for Brave Jack to look like a toy rabbit. He was to stand in the grass without moving, his nose not twitching, tuft of tail not twitching either, eyes not blinking, whiskers stiff, amidst all the make-believe rabbits who were supposed to look real. This he did. He desperately hoped that Old Witch would not pick him out from all the other rabbits who were really toys. The clever real rabbits had flavored the sawdust of the fake ones with bouillon and sage, and had even added a little parsley, so they would taste like stew, Old Witch's favorite dish. But Jack had not seasoned himself with sage and parsley. He had, instead, rubbed himself all over with henbane, a deadly poison, in case Old Witch should grab him. And he did his best to look more like a toy than the real toy ones did, a hard thing for him to do with his heart pounding at the rate of a mile a minute and with the sound of "heh-heh" growing nearer and nearer.

Brave Jack held a little shovel in his hand. With this he was to thump signals to those below. In a panic he went over the signals in his mind. One thump, here Old Witch is. Two thumps, roll rocks in front of entrance way, for she is at it. Three, she is getting in anyway—get ready to fight. Four thumps, Brave Jack himself is in grave danger, and if he does not thump again four times within two minutes, they may have to send up another sentinel. And five, all clear, she's gone.

Brave Jack certainly did have a great deal on his mind. Suppose he mixed up any of the first four with number five! The rabbits would come tumbling out, and there Old Witch would be! Well, he must not think of that and he must not get confused.

Now, having taken in the whole picture and having idled and drooled long enough, suddenly Old Witch swooped down. In a great blow, with gusts of wind that whistled through the pines and tall oaks of the painting field, she came. Frightened birds flew blindly hither and thither, and some, blown against the huge trunks of the oak trees, were knocked unconscious and fell stunned to the ground.

But Old Witch was not interested in knocked-out birds. She was only interested in juicy little fat rabbits and their pretty painted eggs.

Thump! went Jack's shovel, giving the signal that meant, she's here! And, thump! went his heart, and the hearts of all the real, right, regular, alive rabbits down below as they realized that their enemy was riding around above them in the painting field.

"Heh-heh! Hi-hi! he-he! ho-ho!"

What an awful laugh Old Witch had! It could be heard as far away as Garden Lane, where, in the room high up behind the ginkgo tree, Amy, with her friend Clarissa, was still drawing eggs and rabbits and a great old witch in their midst.

It had suddenly grown dark, and the girls had had to turn on the light. "O-o-oh!" said Clarissa. "It's spooky. Did you say that Old Witch catched any rabbits?"

Amy did not answer. "Did you hear that?" she asked solemnly. "*That* sounded like Old Witch. Besides, it's thundering, I think."

So, she and Clarissa got under an old soft rose and blue silk quilt, and they hid.

Meanwhile, in the painting field, Old Witch laughed her "heh-hehs" and "he-he-hes" while swooping here and there, picking up egg after egg (rocks) and ravenously swallowing them whole, eating them as appetizers for the real feast to come—rabbits! She was so greedy and so tired of plain herbs to eat that she did not know the difference between painted rocks and real eggs.

But soon Old Witch became weighted down with the

rock eggs she had eaten and she had trouble keeping her broomstick aloft. She decided, "Enough of the eggs!" They really were not quite as good as she remembered them. Now, for rabbits! She dived down and picked one up, not —thank goodness—Brave Jack, and she ate it, herb-seasoned sawdust and all, with gusto.

Old Witch then ate rabbit after rabbit. Soon she must have eaten about one hundred and one make-believe rabbits, and she was making her way closer and closer to Brave Jack, the lonely sentinel. Now that she was beginning to get filled up, she became more particular about the rabbits she ate. She tried to find the fattest and juiciest ones, the best-seasoned ones. How thankful Jack was that he was not seasoned with sage and parsley! But in her haste and greed Old Witch paid little heed to what sort of rabbit she was eating. She might take a fancy to him, notwithstanding the henbane, he was such a plump and tempting little brown rabbit with such eloquent eyes.

Though a brave rabbit, still Jack quailed when Old Witch swooped down and snatched a toy one just two feet away from him! It had an orange cotton carrot in its mouth, and Old Witch swallowed it, cotton carrot and all, in one loud gulp. Jack was terror-stricken. Old Witch was now at the very entrance way to the cave. It was hard to know whether to give the two-thump signal or the four-thump one. Fortunately, off she swooped, having spotted a rabbit with a crisp bunch of celery in its paws that appealed to her. So, he did not thump at all.

And as if Old Witch were not enough for Jack to have on his mind, he had to consider Tom, too. The witch cat! An old witch, greedy and hungry, may be fooled into thinking that seasoned toy rabbits are real ones, but it is unlikely that a cat, witch or ordinary, can be fooled in this way. And sure enough, the minute Tom had entered the painting field, he had spotted the one real, alive bunny in the picture, Brave Jack!

So, he came sniffing along, dum-de-dum-dum, slowly, deliberately, across the painting field. He stopped at every rabbit he encountered and smelled it thoughtfully and knowingly, as if measuring the amount of sage, say, in it. Then, leaving it untouched, he cleaned his paw, or his ear, and proceeded to the next one. He had but one worry—that possibly Old Witch would grab up the real rabbit before he got to it. Still the game was so delightful that he was willing to take this risk, and he did not race greedily and ignominiously for Jack. Dignity accompanied his thoughtful progress toward his quarry.

But Head Easter Rabbit had laid plans to hoodwink Old Tom as well as Old Witch. He had really thought of every awful possibility. In regard to Tom, this is what he had done. For a distance of about twenty feet in every direction around Brave Jack, the rabbits had scattered catnip in great abundance. Catnip is irresistible to cats, and old witch cat Tom was no exception.

The rain had brought out the fragrance of the catnip, and when Tom reached the twenty-foot line of catnip, he stopped short. Catnip! Tom let out a surprised and de lighted miaow. He rubbed his back lovingly against a huge oak tree, and then he lay down in the catnip. He raised all four of his feet in the air and gave a slow, delicious wallow. What a rolling over in the catnip he had! His head spun pleasantly. At last he staggered to his feet and picked up his slow and roundabout advance toward Jack, whom he had not forgotten in the happy intermission. Along the way, he munched on his unusual delicacy in contentment.

Soon, unable to resist the intoxicating effects of the catnip, he had to stop again and have another roll-himself-over. He ate a few more bites and a few more, and soon he had had a few bites too many. Old Tom, the real, right, regular old witch cat, had become tipsy!

Muddled up, he began to pounce on the toy rabbits, first one and then another. He had trouble remembering what he had been looking for. He lurched against one little toy rabbit that could box, and when Tom fell on it, its mechanics began to work. The boxing rabbit and Tom had a few rounds. This struck Old Tom as hilarious, and he began to laugh. He had what is known as a "laughing jag." The laughter of witch cats is on the order of hyenas', and it is awful. It is hard to know which sounded worse to Jack, Old Tom's hyena-like laughter or Old Witch's breathless "heh-hehs." Tom sank down, and, with his back against the trunk of an oak tree and his legs crossed, he stayed there.

"Oh, the hurly-burly," said Old Witch to Tom as she swept by. Can you believe that this Old Witch was not filled up yet? Now, suddenly, she dived right down on Jack. He felt her hot sage breath on him and nearly fainted with terror. But she smelled the henbane—you can't baffle a witch on herbs—and muttering, "Poison! A trap!" she flung Jack into the brambles.

"Thump! Thump!" went Brave Jack's shovel. He had to let people down below know that he was in the most awful peril they had ever imagined and so were they, for one of Old Witch's feet was almost in the entrance way.

"Roll the rocks against the door!" his signal meant, and this, to a man, they began to do.

But Old Witch had had enough. Slinging her bag of what she thought were rabbits and eggs for the little witches—or, she might change her mind and eat them all herself—over her back, Old Witch boosted sleepy Tom onto the broomstick and up and off and away from the painting field they flew.

Saved! They were all saved! Jack gave five thumps of his shovel and the rabbits thronged out. In exhausted relief, they watched Old Witch soar over the oak trees, homeward bound with the toy rabbits and painted rocks. She had not eaten one live rabbit, or one real painted Easter egg, although, so far, she did not know that she had been duped.

Thankful to be alive, the rabbits sat in a circle and listened to Jack's breath-taking account of the raid. Then they looked sadly about them, taking note of the destruction. So many lovely toy rabbits gone! And if not gone, torn to bits! But better they be gone than real ones. The rabbits would have to work doubly hard to make new toy ones, simple toy ones without mechanical works such as eyes that light up when you press a button, or cymbals to clang. If they expected to have anything ready on time for Easter this year, they would have to create just plain little do-nothing rabbits. But they are very nice, too.

"Good-by, wicked old witch," they shouted.

Old Witch was so weighted down with rocks and rabbits that she barely cleared the ginkgo trees of Garden Lane. But Old Witch did not care.

"Oh, the hurly-burly," she muttered tiredly but happily. "Oh, to glory be!" She pronounced the proper incantation to make her broomstick go higher, for she did not wish to linger on Garden Lane, street of the banquisher, and be discovered in her wickedness.

"Ouch," she said to herself. "My stomach aches."

"THAT BE LIKELY," spelled a somber voice.

Old Witch urged her broomstick to get her to her rickety old front porch and rocker as soon as possible. Creaking and groaning, the broomstick gained a little height. Slowly Old Witch flew away on the return trip home.

Amy and Clarissa peeked out from under the quilt. "The sun's come out," said Amy. "Let's go out and swing." And they did.

CHAPTER ELEVEN

The Picnic at the Mermaid Lagoon

While Old Witch had been engaged in her delightful rabbit wickedness in the painting field, Little Witch Girl and little Weeny Witchie had been on a pretty picnic with no witch wickedness involved.

"Would you like me to take you to the mermaid lagoon?" Little Witch Girl had asked Weeny Witchie in low, crooning tones.

"Cr-cr-cr," gurgled Beebee, moistening her lips and shaking a few sparks out of her fingers.

Guessing that these little croaks and sparks meant "yes," the little witch girl gave Beebee a hug. Then she said she would pack a surprise picnic for the little mermaid and *her* baby sister. She made sandwiches out of herbs. These may not sound very good to you, but the little witch girl was used to them and knew nothing about hot dogs and potato chips. She also packed a bottle of herb formula for Beebee.

The weather was stormy, but this does not matter to witches. In fact, they like it. And the stormy weather provided Little Witch Girl with a good excuse to put Beebee's little black bunny suit on her. Beebee screamed and kicked and grew red in the face while she was being tucked into it. But when all was over and she was as warm and snug as she could be, she said "Abr" happily. Little Witch Girl straightened out Beebee's witch hat and all was ready.

She strapped Beebee onto her broomstick and climbed on herself. She held tightly to her little sister, and in this safe fashion they slowly glided down the glass hill to the secret opening. Then slowly they flew down the magical passageway to the mermaid lagoon.

There, by the pool, they saw Lurie. She was singing gently and rocking Babay in her lap. "One little, two little, three little mermaids," she sang. "Oh!" she exclaimed, interrupting her song. "Is that your little sister?"

Little Witch Girl nodded proudly. "Her name be Beebee!" she said.

"She be cute!" said the little mermaid, and she helped Little Witch Girl to get Beebee out of her bunny suit. Beebee objected to this as much as she had at being put into it. But when they laid Weeny Witchie on a smooth pink rock, hollowed out as though by the sea, she said "Abr" again very happily.

"Just doesn't like to get in and out of bunny suits," explained Little Witch Girl to the little mermaid.

They put the mermaid baby in a shallow pool next to Beebee, and she splashed her hands and her tail in the water. Beebee liked the sight and shook out some sparks for the little mermaid. Both gurgled happily throughout the picnic.

"I hoped you would come today," the little mermaid said. "Isn't it real witch weather outside? I can tell because of the light in here." Without sun shining through, and without its usual myriads of pure colors, the glass hill seemed like a pearl, a dreamy, misty pearl.

Little Witch Girl nodded. How lovely it was to be here, she thought.

Then she and the little mermaid spread out the picnic on a large, flat white rock. Little Witch Girl and Beebee had never tasted sardines before, but they thought they were very good. As for the little mermaid, she enjoyed the herb sandwiches, which, she claimed, were on the order of sea-weed ones. She picked off some pretty colored crystals from the wall for everyone to suck on for dessert, and these tasted like rock candy.

"How beautiful it is in here!" said the little witch girl. "How quiet!" she breathed.

Quiet! At this moment, from far away at the end of the glass passageway, horrible croaks and gasps and incantations and puffs and abracadabras and "up-you-go's" and grunts could suddenly be heard.

"Oh!" exclaimed Little Witch Girl in terror. Was Old Witch on her way in here? Had she discovered the secret of the glass hill, this place of enchantment deep within it? She might eat up the little mermaid and Babay in hopes they were fish!

Weeny Witchie recognized the voice of her beloved old gammer Old Witch and crowed happily. "Abr, abr, abr," she squealed to make her gammer hear, and she sent a shower of sparks down the passageway.

However, Babay did not like the awful sounds, and she cried piteously. The little mermaid had to take her up in her arms and croon to her. And Little Witch Girl quickly clasped Weeny Witchie's hands together so she could not send any more sparks afloat down the tunnel and give away the secret of the lagoon to Old Witch.

At last the grunts, croaks, gasps, and incantations sounded fainter. Old Witch must be leaving. With her going, the black clouds outside apparently lifted. Twinkling colors gradually reappeared inside the lagoon; the sun was probably coming out; and it was time for the little witches to go home.

The little mermaid gave each of the little witches a piece of blue and red glass to look through. Beebee gurgled happily and, being distracted at the view of the pool through red glass, she did not object to being put into her hot black bunny suit and tied onto the broomstick.

Little Witch Girl gave Beebee loving little squeezes as they flew slowly down the path to the entranceway and then up and away to the top of the hill. There, at the edge of the hill, an odd sight met their eyes. Old Witch was having a terrible time trying to get her broomstick with Tom, asleep on it, over the nob of the hill.

"Oh, there you are, my dears!" she gasped. "Something's gone wrong with my broomstick. Needs oil. Take this sack. It's very precious. But it's too heavy for my broomstick. Getting old, that's what's happening to my broomstick! O-old!" Old Witch gave a mighty groan.

Little Witch Girl landed her broomstick on top of the glass hill and then hoisted up the old witch's heavy-laden shawl. Relieved of this weight, the old broomstick carried Old Witch and Tom up and over the top, and everybody reached home safely. Old Witch, with her precious shawl on her lap, sank into her rickety rocker and rocked. Tom, still sleeping soundly, lay at her feet, a silly grin on his face.

With Beebee in her arms, Little Witch Girl tiptoed over to Malachi. "How be everything?" she whispered.

Gravely he gave his answer. "WICKEDNESS BE AFOOT!" A frown puckered his blunt face. "PLEDGES BE BROKEN!" he said, and said no more.

It was enough. Little Witch Girl put Beebee, still in her bunny suit, on the floor in the sunny corner of the porch near watchful Malachi. She herself sat down in her little red rocker right next to Old Witch who was rocking in her own rickety old rocker. Out of the corner of her eye, Little Witch Girl looked at old gammer Old Witch to see if she looked any different after wickedness than she had before. Old Witch was rocking tiredly and without her usual vigor. Little Witch Girl heard her mutter, "What a magnificent day! Oh, to glory be!" Then she muttered, "Too highly seasoned!" She looked as though she did not feel very well.

Apparently Old Witch did not feel as well as she thought she should after such a splendid feast of eggs and rabbits. After rocking a bit longer and feeling no better, she said, "Come here, my dear. Open up my shawl and see what I have." Since she had such an awful stomach-ache, Old Witch had decided to give all the eggs and rabbits she had stolen to the little witches. Somehow, she did not feel like eating any more of them herself.

"See?" she said.

Little Witch Girl emptied the contents of the shawl into Old Witch's lap—the rock eggs and the toy rabbits. Then, for the first time, Old Witch saw that the eggs were rocks, hand-painted rocks, and that the rabbits had sawdust and ticking inside of them and were toys, not real. When she saw how the clever rabbits had flavored the toy bunnies with sage and parsley, she grew very angry. No one likes to be made a fool of, and this had certainly happened to her.

"BEFOOLED," spelled a calm voice nearby.

This put Old Witch into a frenzy. "I'll go back to the painting field!" she screeched. "I'll get the real rabbits! There won't be one live rabbit left this time. Oh, to glory be!" She staggered to her feet, prepared to create an even more terrible hurly-burly than before. But she immediately sank back into her rocker. She was too weak, and she had too bad a stomach-ache. How did this defeat impress Little Witch Girl, she wondered, casting a glance in her direction. What she saw was a look of enchantment spreading over the face of the little witch girl.

Aside from the tiny doll, Little Lydia, the little witch

girl did not own any pretty toys. Now, here were beauti-ful hand-painted rocks and many toy rabbits.

Old Witch gave a shrug. Well, all had not been in vain. "When you think of it," she assured herself, "the raid on the painting field may really be looked upon as an expedition to get toys for the little ones. Heh-heh!" She laughed feebly. Absent-mindedly she kept blinking the eyes of one of the toy rabbits that lighted up when she pressed a button.

Little Witch Girl waked up Beebee to see. "Cr-cr-cr," gurgled Beebee. Old Witch picked out a pretty little rock with the head of a rabbit painted on it for Beebee to teethe on. The other rocks she gave to Little Witch Girl. On some of the rocks, the Head Rabbit had painted heads of cherubs, lions, gnomes, kittens, and dogs. Little Witch Girl made a border of these around the porch, where they looked very pretty and brightened up the bare and bleak glass hill. "If we had a pool with grass around it—grass, not glass—a real little pool, and flowers—real flowers—and trees . . . wouldn't these rocks be pretty then, shining in the pool and in the grass then?"

Old Witch felt worse and worse. The worse she felt, the more brooding she became about the events of the day. She had reason to brood, having broken the strict rule never-more to go down off the glass hill. Would Amy forbid her to be the real and right Halloween witch? As things had turned out, the trip had really not been worth such a price. She had been made a fool of, and her stomach hurt.

It did not make her feel any better to hear a taunting voice spell out, "HOW MANY B'S BE THERE IN RABBIT?"

Old Witch tucked the thought away in the back of her mind that Malachi had been the cause of her failure in the painting field. "I be outwitted by a bee," thought Old Witch, and felt worse than ever. At this moment when she was feeling her very, very worst, the red cardinal bird flew up and dropped a letter in Old Witch's lap. "Here's the bad news," muttered Old Witch, thinking, of course, banquishment rules had been stiffened. She opened up the little wad of a letter and read:

"Dear Old Witchie,
    Don't worry. You did not eat the rabbits. You did not eat the eggs either. You were bad, but not too bad. Never come down again though, or—no Halloweeny! If you never come down again and scare the rabbits, and if you be good, then you can still be the Halloween witch.

> I love you and you love me,
> Amy."

Old Witch felt so relieved that she felt better right away. "Oh, to glory be!" she muttered and she fell asleep. When she waked up, she felt fine and did not have a stomach-ache any more. She felt so much improved that she was able to pay attention to a plan that began to buzz around in her head—a plan to get the better of Malachi. Her defeat still stung deeply into her pride.

"Heh-heh-heh," she sang softly as she rocked and turned the eyes of the mechanical rabbit off and on, off and on in the twilight. "There be a way to outwit the spelling bee," she sang. "And I be the one to do it. Confront him, confute him, confound him, confuse him. . . . Tum-Tee-Tee-Tum," she sang.

"BEEMENTED!" was the comment she heard, and it stiffened her resolve.

CHAPTER TWELVE

The Spelling Bee

Amy was swinging on the fuzzy little rope swing tied to the small fir tree in the front yard. It was not a very comfortable swing, but Amy had put a little pillow in it so the rope would not cut into her legs. At times it was her favorite swing, for she did not like always to swing in the bought back-yard swing. Here she loved to swing and dream. Here, sometimes, she waited for Clarissa to come running up the street. And here in the summertime—as it was now—she could watch the bees swarming in and out of their nests in the hard ground beneath her where the ivy did not grow.

"I would like to see the Queen bee—if she sits on a throne," thought Amy drowsily, watching the busy bees. Perhaps Malachi, before he became magic and her representative in the witch family, used to live in this bee nest below her, she thought. Maybe he was the duke. Maybe a great wind had blown him into the back yard away from his home in the front. And now he was way away, on top of the glass hill, keeping his eyes on Old Witch, outwitting her in her wickedness. Duke Malachi! Never before had there been a bee as big and as important as Malachi.

Since it was summertime now, perhaps Malachi would

come down for a little visit. "He has probably eaten up all the honey stored inside all the little rooms of his stomach. His private pantry filled with . . ."

"HONEY!" gently hummed a bee close to her ear.

Since there was only one real spelling bee that Amy knew of, this must be Malachi! Buzzing busily, he flew past her and alighted on a large pink clover, his favorite kind, at the edge of the little square front yard. The big bumblebee, no longer looking like dry winter wheat, was all puffed out and as golden and beautiful as fresh acacia.

"He's filling up with honey to live on while he's keeping his eyes on Old Witch," thought Amy. She watched him go from flower to flower, from the tall pink clover to the little white clovers, and then to the honeysuckle next door.

There was quite a buzzing among all the bees who, no doubt, were discussing Malachi's arrival. But Malachi's loud buzzing could be heard above that of all the others, for he buzzed out words. "GOOD," he spelled, and "HOT!" and "CAN'T STAY LONG!" and "HAVE TO WATCH WITCH!" and "ON GUARD!" and "GOOD MUST WIN!"

"Practicing his spelling," thought Amy. If she had had paper and pencil, she would have written down the words of the bee to show Clarissa.

As soon as they saw that the big and patriarchal bumblebee did not intend to visit them, the workers on the ground, the ordinary nonspelling bees, became too busy to pay further attention to Malachi. He went on with his spelling and they with their gathering of honey. It was very hot. The sweet, drowsy droning of the bees made Amy sleepy. Her eyes almost closed. The tranquillity was that of a perfect summer day. The sky was Amy's favorite shade of blue.

Sometimes through her drooping lashes, she saw Malachi, a golden sunny blur close by, against this limpid blue. It was as though only she and Malachi inhabited the earth. Her eyes closed and opened and closed and opened. It was hard to stay awake.

Malachi! Sleepily Amy watched him. He was balanced again atop the swaying large pink clover. Now he seemed to be searching for something else, not honey, something in his mind. "He has all his many eyes on me," thought Amy.

"What be ye doing, Malachi," asked Amy, "sitting on that clover, not gathering honey?"

"I BE SEARCHING FOR THE RIGHT WORD," answered Malachi.

"Oh," said Amy. "You know that Old Witch is very angry with you and is just bemented to find you?"

"YES," he spelled.

"She be going to challenge you to a battle of the wits," said Amy. "But I be sure you will win."

"WHEN?" asked Malachi. No longer did he sound like a relaxed bumblebee happily gathering honey or words on a hot summer day. He sounded grave, like a bumblebee foreboding trouble and anxious to avert it.

"As soon as you get back," said Amy.

Amy grew wide awake too, for at this moment there came a far distant rumbling of thunder.

"WITCH!" spelled Malachi. He alighted for a moment on Amy's left hand that tightly grasped the fuzzy rope. He let her touch his soft plush back.

"Would 'befuddle' be the right word you were searching for?" Amy asked softly.

"MIGHT BE! I GO!" he said.

"w i n!" Amy implored him, spelling the word. And Malachi flew away home, just as Clarissa ran up.

Clarissa had a cool sun suit on—blue. But Amy's dress was as golden as Malachi. Clarissa's little round face was beady and hot. "I wish we could go to the Oldtown swimming pool," she said.

"I do too," said Amy. "But who would take us?"

"No one," said Clarissa.

"No one," said Amy. "Well, come on in. It's too hot to stay out. Did you see Malachi?"

"N O N," spelled Clarissa. Spelling the words was a habit both she and Amy were getting into. And Clarissa, having been born in Paris, France, could spell three words in French. Non. That means no. Oui. That means yes. And papillon. That means butterfly. Oui, non, papillon—a very pretty rhyme.

They went upstairs to Amy's mother's cool high-ceilinged room shaded by the lovely summery ginkgo tree. "Let's draw," said Amy.

"Yes," said Clarissa. "But first, I am going to play, 'How Much Is That Doggie in the Window?' " She put on this record and she sat in front of the Victrola and she rocked in Amy's little red rocker.

But Amy began to draw right away. In her picture she put Old Witch gazing into a crystal ball.

Now Old Witch really was looking in her crystal ball. She had given up searching in her runes for clues to outwit Malachi, for she found nothing that had to do with the case. Instead she spent the long hot summer days consulting her crystal ball. She hoped a picture would appear in it that would reveal to her how she might outwit Malachi. She blamed all her disgraceful defeats on Malachi, and the fiasco in the painting field had been the last straw. But in the crystal ball she always saw the same thing—just the big old bumblebee staring out at her as though admonishing her. And the crystal ball never revealed his whereabouts. Discouraged though she was, Old Witch kept peering in the ball. And that was what she was still doing when Malachi, the spelling bee, sped back to his camouflage place at the sunny end of the porch. Of course, being camouflage, this place could not show in crystal balls.

Suddenly a look of great interest came over Old Witch's face. Apparently there was a change in the crystal ball. Words were appearing in it.

"What be them words?" Old Witch asked herself.

At first the words were very tiny. But they grew larger and clearer, and finally she could read them clearly. This she did, aloud.

"Search not for the bumblebee.
   He'll sting and sting and sting, Nobby!
   Know'st thou not how to outwit him?
   Forsooth, then know'st thou must outspell him!"

"Heh-heh!" screeched Old Witch in horrid glee. "A spelling bee! A spelling bee!"

She screeched so loudly that she waked up Beebee. But Beebee did not mind. She clapped her hands happily and sent out sparks. "A bee, a bee," she said.

"Spelling," said Old Witch proudly.

But Little Witch Girl's heart had jumped into her throat. She thought Old Witch had captured Malachi! Fortunately, a swift glance at the camouflage place assured her that no such thing had happened. "Now, my dearie dear," said Old Witch. There was something in Old Witch's tone—a certain conniving note—that the little witch girl did not like and that filled her with dread. "We are going to have a spelling bee, your bumblebee friend and I, the head witch. The little witches from the witch school must come, for otherwise it is not a true bee. They are going to see that I am no longer going to be bit, bullied, and outwitted by a bumblebee."

"Oh, my!" said Little Witch Girl.

Old Witch then stood on the tiptop of the glass hill and

she croaked three terrible hoarse and horrible croaks. Led by the witch schoolteacher, the six little witches from witch school flew up on their broomsticks. "What's up?" they wondered in excitement. They were very happy to have this interesting summons from the witch house of exile to break the dullness of the hot and humid day. They did not have to wait long for an answer.

"As you know," Old Witch said, "there has been a great deal of trouble with a certain bee, Malachi, known as the spelling bee. I am going to put an end to this trouble. A spelling bee is about to take place between myself and this mumble, this humble, this bumble bee. (Here there was much laughter at her sneering tone, and snickering.) It be now my intention to outspell the spelling bee. Once out-spelled, his magic will be gone, heh-heh! Be there a better speller than I be?" she asked the little witches.

"No! There be not!" they all screeched together.

"BEEHOLD!" spelled a scornful, powerful, buzzing voice.

"Pay no heed to that," said Old Witch. "We'll go on with the plans. You three (and she picked out Tweet, and Itch and Twitch, the twins) sit on this side. You other three (and here she picked out Notesy, Olie, and Izzy) sit oppo-site. Schoolteacher, you be the umpire and sit at that end. I, myself, will stand at this end. Malachi be where he be."

Little Witch Girl would not join in the game, for she loved both contestants. She secretly hoped that Malachi would win, however. She knew that if he won, he would not hurt Old Witch very much. But if Old Witch won, she did not like to think what Old Witch might do to him.

Old Witch scribbled some words on a sheet of paper and handed it to the witch teacher. Then she went to her end

of the porch and did a weird backanally to ready herself
for the word battle with the bee. Her backanally was interesting to all. But more interesting than it to the witch
teacher was a new word that hopped by magic onto her
list of spelling words. "Hm-m-m," said the witch teacher,
bemused.

Her backanally finished, Old Witch was about to tell the
witch teacher to sound the gong and call the first word
when the same buzzing, warning voice as before spelled,
"B E E G I N!"

Everybody jumped. Of course they could not see Malachi, and every time he spoke, his voice seemed to come
from a different direction. "A ventriloquist bumblebee,"
thought Little Witch Girl proudly.

"Took the word right out of my mouth," said Old
Witch, chagrined.

"Well," comforted the witch schoolteacher. "If the bumblebee continues to spell like that, he will certainly never
win."

"B E E   S T I L L!" commanded the voice.

"Heh-heh!" laughed Old Witch, reassured. "Two e's in
be—that be wrong."

Of course Malachi was just trying to get Old Witch
mixed up, the little witch girl thought, putting more e's in
every word than there should be.

"All right, then," screeched Old Witch. "We shall *bee*-
gin. Give the first word, schoolteacher. Let the bee *bee*-
gin."

The little witch girl hastily cautioned Malachi. "Remember," she said softly, "to spell the words backward and not
forward, or the teacher will count you wrong."

"S E Y," said Malachi, who certainly could spell backward

as well as forward. This is a hard and strict way to spell, but witches think that if you can spell backward, you can then certainly spell going forward, the easy way.

The first word was a trick, to try and confuse the bumblebee.

"Bee!" commanded the teacher. "Spell 'Hannah.'"

"HANNAH!" spelled Malachi slowly and distinctly, and not in the least nervous.

But Old Witch screeched, "He has put the wrong H first. There should be a small h first. He has spelled Hannah the wrong way around. Count him wrong, count him wrong," she screamed.

"He spelled it right," said three of the little witches.

"He spelled it wrong," said the other three.

"PROVE IT," said Malachi calmly.

"The capital H comes last!" screamed the witch.

"I SPEAK ONLY IN CAPITALS," said Malachi with dignity.

"He speaks only in capitals," said all the little witches in awe. "What a bee!" And all agreed, "Last is first and first is last. He spelled it right."

The umpire teacher, too, said that Malachi had won on that catch word, for she was a fair witch, at least as fair as they came. "Next word," she said. "Your turn, Mistress Nobby," she said with a courteous croak. "Spell . . . bumblebee."

Old Witch began well enough. "eebelbmu," she said, but at the end she said, "bee."

"Wrong for the right way," said the witch teacher.

"WRONG," said Malachi severely, "FOR ANYWAY!" And he said, "TWO DOWN."

Old Witch was very angry. Thomp! She stomped up

and down the porch. The little witches were glad that she was not angry with any of them. "Give her another chance," they said.

"Very well," said the witch teacher. "Spell 'befuddle,'" she said. This was the word that Malachi had added to the list by magic.

Now Malachi had put so many extra e's in every word that had "be" in it that Old Witch was truly becoming befuddled. In her ears there was the sound as of the swarming of bees. She began, "elddufe," and then she made another mistake and put the extra e in again, and so the word came out "beefuddle."

"Bees in her bonnet," thought schoolteacher irreverently. The little witches all gasped. "She really is befuddled," they said.

Fire flew from Old Witch's eyes. Thunder and lightning filled the air. She stomped back and forth in fury. "Spell 'witch,'" she screamed. (If 'witch' is misspelled, all the most wicked and loathsome witches there are in the world will appear and do what Old Witch says to do.)

Slowly and distinctly, craftily and deliberately, Malachi began. "H C T I," he spelled. Then he paused as though searching for the next and right letter. Old Witch could not help laughing, "Heh-heh." Now so far, what clever Malachi had spelled of the word was 'itch.' Curiously enough at this point, Old Witch began scratching herself. The more she scratched the more she itched. She seemed to itch all over.

"Say the W, say the W," she beseeched. But Malachi would not.

It was a comical sight to see Old Witch try to reach the

middle of her back. The little witches all enjoyed it until they too began to itch. All the little witches had caught the itches, and when the umpire schoolteacher witch also began to itch, she and the little ones all flew away, screaming with laughter, and each one trying to scratch the back of the one in front. "He BEE the winner," they taunted Old Witch as they rode away.

"I WON," said Malachi simply.

To warn Old Witch not to try to get the better of him again, Malachi poured honey all over the porch where she was stomping. Her feet got stuck in it like flies to flypaper, and she could not get loose. The honey was as magic as Malachi, having been stored in his magic stomach. So, Old Witch had to stay stuck. She bent low in every direction trying to break loose, but she could not. She began to regret having stirred up trouble with a spelling bee.

Then, out of kindness, Malachi finished spelling the word. "W," he said. The minute he put the W onto witch, Old Witch stopped itching and stopped being stuck in the honey. She sat down in her old wicker rocker. "Oh, to glory be," she thought. "Outwitted me again. But I'll get him yet," she said in fury. "I will."

"MIND YOUR OWN BEESWAX," said Malachi. This was the first time that Malachi had ever made a joke, and he buzzed heartily. Naturally, he felt lighthearted, having achieved such a telling victory.

Down below, at the yellow table, Clarissa laughed out loud at the way Amy had drawn Old Witch, in a horizontal position, trying to unstick herself from the honey. "Malachi should have left her there," she said.

"What!" said Amy. "And us have no Halloween witch?

Nope! Anyway, Little Witch Girl would not have liked that. Would you like to see your grandmother stuck to the floor, forever, in honey?" she asked Clarissa solemnly.

"My grandmother is in Tangiers," said Clarissa. "How many times do I have to tell you?"

"But if she were not in Tangiers, would you like to have her stuck in honey?"

"n o," spelled Clarissa.

"Well, then. Neither would Little Witch Girl. And who would cook the herbs and make the soup? Just a little sticking—that was long enough."

"Oh," groaned Clarissa. "I feel sticky! If only we could go swimming in the Oldtown swimming pool!"

"M-m-m," said Amy. "That'd be nice."

CHAPTER THIRTEEN

The Great Night at Last

"You know what tonight is, don't you?" said Amy, wagging her finger wisely at Clarissa.

Clarissa looked knowing. But the truth was, she had forgotten. Her memory was not very long. Often the most she could remember was whether there was school today or not. Then it came to her in a flash, the way the right answer sometimes pops into your head in arithmetic, and you don't quite know where the answer came from—some deep down inside-the-head secret storing place for answers, probably.

"I know," she said. "It's Halloween. And we go tricksing and treating."

It was Saturday. Amy and Clarissa were at the little table, drawing large pictures of pumpkins, ghosts, black cats, and witches—big and little witches, baby witches, and witch dolls. Their papers were covered with witches flying in front of huge moons.

"And," Amy went on, "you know that tonight Old Witch can get off the glass hill and come right down here, even to Garden Lane, if she wants to?" She looked sharply at Clarissa to see if she had taken in this important reminder.

"She can!" exclaimed Clarissa. "Even though she came down for the rabbits and the eggs?"

"Yes," answered Amy solemnly. "Even though. You know why? Because she didn't eat one real rabbit, just toy rabbits, and she didn't eat the real painted eggs, just plain painted rocks. So I wrote her—don't you remember anything?—and told her she could come down for Halloween."

"Oh yes, of course," said Clarissa.

"So she can. What is the use of Halloween without Old Witch? No use."

"Of course not," said Clarissa.

"But I am S C A R E D!" spelled Amy.

"I'm N O T," said Clarissa.

"Well, *I'm* scared because we might see Old Witch when we go tricksing and treating. She might not like me because I banquished her to the top of the glass hill to learn to be good. And one thing, Clarissa. You know one thing, don't you?"

"No," said Clarissa.

"Witches do not like to be good. They hate it."

"Well, Amy," said Clarissa. "We are going to be with Polly and Christopher Knapp. We won't be scared because Chris is nine."

"That's right," said Amy, hoping she would be a brave girl and not mind about Old Witch. "Will you come for me?" she asked.

"Oh yes, of course. I'll come for you," Clarissa promised.

Amy surveyed her scary drawing. "Clarissa," she said, "you better go home now and get ready."

"Now!" said Clarissa. "Get ready now! It's morning now. We have to wait for nighttime to put on our costumes and go out."

Amy sat back and thought. "Yes," she said. "It has to be dark, very dark. And the sky must be the Halloween sky. And the moon must be the Halloween moon. And the clouds, the Halloween clouds. Everything will be scary and spooky and windy. I guess Little Witch Girl is getting ready now."

"And Weeny Witchie." Clarissa laughed.

"Weeny Witchie! Are you a nope?" said Amy. "Weeny Witchie can't come. She's too little. She might get lost. Maybe even Little Witch Girl can't come. She might have to stay home and mind Beebee. Old Witch might have planned to leave Little Witch Girl home even if there wasn't a baby in the family. Does your mother, or your grandmother, take you everywhere she goes?"

"Grandmother! She is in Tangiers."

"Well, do they take you everywhere they go?'

"No."

"Well, it is the same with witches. They don't take their little witch girls everywhere they go either. What do you think the witch family is doing right this minute?" asked Amy. "Probably carving awful punkins," she answered herself.

She was right.

Old Witch and Little Witch Girl were carving awful pumpkins at that minute. Since pumpkins did not grow on the bare and bleak glass hill, Old Witch had got them by means of abracadabra—a terrible huge pumpkin head for herself, a terrible medium-sized one for the little witch girl, and a tiny, terrible one for Weeny Witchie.

Old Witch and Little Witch Girl were on the rickety porch, stooping over the pumpkins, scooping them out, and carving terrible faces. The more terrible the face, the more delightedly Weeny Witch croaked. All the while they were muttering runes, chants, and abracadabras, in order to get the right Halloween magic into the air. This magic would spread out all over the world, and boys and girls everywhere would feel it and know that soon it would be Halloween night and that they must shiver and shake.

"Some don't look hard enough," thought Old Witch glumly. She liked to be seen. What is the use of being the Halloween witch and not being seen?

"May I go down tonight?" asked the little witch girl. "Please, please, please say yes. I'd love to be seen on my broomstick in the light of the moon."

"No, no," croaked Old Witch amiably. "You must stay home with Beebee."

"Why can't Wee Tommy cat mind his own weeny witchie?"

"Too wee," said Old Witch. "That's why. You must stay here, my dear," she said with a slight cackle, which sounded quite unpleasant.

Little Witch Girl began to cry.

Old Witch did not care, for today was her day for wickedness. The more tears the merrier, she thought, and she laughed her awful "heh-heh."

Little Witch Girl sobbed softly. She had set her heart on flying down tonight to see her friends, Amy and Clarissa. They were one of the main reasons she wanted to go on the hurly-burly.

"Well," she said to herself rebelliously. "I am going."

On this one day, she could be wicked too. Being wicked was not reserved just for Old Witch. It was for all witches, big, little, and weeny ones. As she carved and scooped and made the scary face, she began to think up a plan. She dried her eyes as hope took root.

Carving the pumpkins was now finished. Old Witch let Beebee have the pleasure of lighting them with her sparks. Then they placed the big terrible one (Old Witch's) on the post of the front porch, the medium-sized terrible one (Little Witch Girl's) in the front window, and the tiny terrible one (Weeny Witch's) on the hearth.

Nighttime came. Wind began to howl. Hobgoblins filled the air. The moon rose and, like a true Halloween moon, now it disappeared behind the swift swirling clouds, and now it came out again. Vapors came and vapors vanished. A cat appeared from somewhere with nine tails, and disappeared again—in the vapors. Old Tom let out his long Halloween howl, walked thrice around the grand pumpkin, ran to Old Witch's grand broomstick, and lashed his one tail nine times forth and nine times back.

Then Old Witch mounted her broomstick, true witch sideways style, and muttered the appropriate incantation. Old Tom leaped on. His back was arched and his hair was bristling in the true Halloween cat style. Away and up and off they flew, on their way to the saturnalia, which is a place for witch wickedness.

"Oh, the hurly-burly!" the little witch girl heard Old Witch screech as she flew away.

The minute that Old Witch was out of sight, Little Witch Girl picked up Beebee and put her bunny suit on her. She was going to be wicked and disobey Old Witch. Otherwise, why be a witch? She was going to visit Amy and Clarissa—return their party call. "That is only politeness, isn't it?" she said to Beebee.

Beebee said, "Abr, abr, abr," seeming to agree.

What the little Witch Girl planned to do was to ask the little mermaid to mind Beebee for her while she was away.

First Little Witch Girl felt in the hem of her cloak for the Malachi rune, for of course she would not embark upon such an expedition as this without that important clipping. It was there, all right. Then she said, "Good-by," to Malachi. He answered, "BE CAREFUL!" And then she strapped Weeny Witchie to her broomstick and sailed down to the mermaid lagoon. Of course they took their cats with them.

The little mermaid happened to be waiting for them with Halloween treats. You are not best friends of a witch without having picked up some of the customs. The treats were very nice, pretty pebbles, delicate shells, and crystal candies.

"Will you mind Beebee for me?" asked the little witch girl.

"I'd love to," said the little mermaid.

"And please keep these pretty treats for me until I get back," said the little witch girl.

"Oh yes," said the little mermaid.

"Good-by then," said Little Witch Girl.

The little mermaid flipped her tail sadly. She would have

liked to go too. But of course she couldn't, for she could not stay on the broomstick. Moreover, being a mermaid, she had to plunge into the pool now and then to cool off. "Good-by," she murmured. "Have a good time," she said, giving the little witch girl a sweet smile, not to spoil her fun. Anyway, she had two babies to watch out for, and to play with, and keep her company, so she was not sad for very long.

Little Witch Girl gave the little mermaid and the two babies a kiss and a hug. Then she mounted her broomstick. She uttered the most complicated runes that her class had studied so far. Some small hobgoblins appeared. "Don't be frightened," she said to the little mermaid. The hobgoblins escorted her down the narrow glass path, alight with moon glow. Little Tommy miaowed happily.

"Ah, the hulie-bulie," said the little witch girl, trying to sound awful like Old Witch. But she didn't sound awful. She just sounded like herself, the little witch girl.

The moon was racing across the heavens, weaving in and out of the clouds. And now, at last, the little witch girl could be seen against the bouncy full moon as she steered her broomstick down and down and down toward Garden Lane where important happenings were taking place—the Halloween happenings of Amy and Clarissa.

CHAPTER FOURTEEN

Halloween on Garden Lane

Down on Garden Lane, a group of boys and girls—Amy and Clarissa, Polly Knapp and her brother Christopher, who, being nine, was the main man of the expedition—had just gathered together on Amy's front stoop. They were about to go from house to house and ring doorbells and say, "Trick or treat."

Anyone would have trouble recognizing them. Clarissa was a little Chinese girl, dressed in a pale pink pajama costume, silk, and she had make-up on her face. Amy was a—you know what—little witch girl. One might think he could recognize her by the long blond hair hanging down below her black witch hat. But she had such a terrible scary witch false face on, no one could be sure. She carried a little broomstick with her, but of course she could not get it up in the air, not being a real witch.

Polly Knapp? Who would ever guess her? She was a black cat, and not one inch of Polly showed. Christopher was a frightening red devil, and not one inch of him showed either. Some tiny little children of about three were tagging along, too. These must be the Epes children who lived across the street. They were probably three, four, and five years old, though they were all about the same size in their

hobgoblin costumes. All the children had enormous bags for "trick or treat."

Halloween shadows played upon the walls of the houses. In the sky the Halloween moon raced in and out of clouds. The Halloween wind was blowing, not a blasting of wind but a right-sized swelling, falling, and gushing of wind. It was a lovely and exciting night, exactly the kind of night Halloween should be. Amy's rapture was complete. She looked up at the sky.

"See that witch?" she asked Clarissa. She pointed to the moon in front of which she happened to have been lucky enough to see Old Witch riding, on her way to her saturnalia. At least Amy thought that she had seen her. Old Witch had flown by so fast, she was a little uncertain.

"No," said Clarissa.

This answer made Amy certain. "Well, I saw her. It was Old Witch," she said solemnly.

It was time to start. "Come on," summoned Chris Knapp. "Let's go."

First they ran up the steps of Polly and Chris Knapp's house, next door to Amy's. The entire house was in darkness. But when the children knocked and said, "Trick or treat!" the door slowly opened, an inch at a time, a lighted pumpkin head appeared gradually, and a terribly scary voice, like that of a real witch said, "Ooooh, ooooh, ooooh!"

All the children fell back. Pretend witch Amy almost fell over, she was so scared. "Oh!" she said when she recognized Polly Knapp's pretty mother. "You scared we!"

Polly's mother dropped something that smelled very good and spicy into their big brown bags, and the children rushed away—but not to the next house. In the next house there lived a very cross and mean old woman. The children did not like to see this old woman on ordinary days, let alone on Halloween, because she was a keeper of toys. Let a ball or a kite go over her fence and land in her yard, and she kept it, just plain kept it for good. She did not like children and thought they were all hobgoblins whether it was Halloween or not. She kept their toys to teach them not to let their things come flying over her fence.

"She could at least give them back," said Amy in disgust. "She does not have to smile, but she could at least give them back. Not just keep them!" she said.

The children fled to the next house, for they thought they saw the old woman's beady black eyes watching them through her dark shutters.

Garden Lane was only one short block long. Tonight

the children must not go off it. There was a lamppost in the middle of it and one at each end. Between the lampposts, and beneath the high ginkgo trees that lined both sides of the street, it was dark and mysterious. At one end, Garden Lane joined another street. At the other end there was a beautiful spacious estate with tall oak trees, thick shrubbery, and soft grass upon which the moon cast a pale, elusive light as it came in and out of the clouds.

"What a wonderful garden for witches!" thought Amy. She was glad that Chris did not lead them into that garden for trick or treat. She did not want to see Old Witch in that garden. Seeing Old Witch against the moon, flying high on her broomstick, was all right. But not down on Garden Lane!

The excitement and joy of the night quickened Amy's heartbeat, and she looked up and all around. And there! She was sure she saw her again—Old Witch sailing by again. Being in charge of the entire Halloween all over the world was keeping Old Witch very busy, of course. She would not have one plain girl, Amy, on her mind. That was what Amy hoped anyway. Once Amy was sure she heard her "heh-heh" and once "Oh, to glory be!"

The children kept going up one stoop and down another. In the light of the street lamp they looked like real little ghoulies, witches, goblins, and black cats. Their bags were becoming so full of apples, popcorn, Tootsie Rolls, cookies, and pennies that the children were staggering.

"Oh-o-oh, my!" they exclaimed as they peered into their bags in the circle of light around the middle lamppost. This middle lamppost stood in front of a pretty little brick house that was painted gray. The bright red door of this little house was the one they planned to knock at next.

Being rather shy, Amy was always the last one to run up the steps to the door, never the first or even the second. She was not at all like Chris Knapp, the leader, or brave Clarissa, or even quiet Polly Knapp who shouted "Trick or treat!" as loudly as the rest. Polly felt quite brave inside her cat costume because you could not see one inch of her and say, "Hello, Polly Knapp." But Amy was just as shy inside her witch costume as she was out of it. This was why she was always the last to run up the steps and into other people's houses.

That was what happened now, at the little gray house. The others all ran up the steps, rang the bell, and called lustily. Amy was about to tag along with the littlest ones—the hobgoblins and the ghoulies—when she had to stop short in her tracks under the lamppost.

She thought she saw Little Witch Girl flying up their very own street named Garden Lane on her broomstick! She did see her! She was sure of it! She saw her very clearly now, by the light of the middle lamppost. Little Witch Girl had her little black cat Tommy with her. His back was arched and his mouth was open in the Halloween manner.

Rooted to the sidewalk at this startling sight, Amy, naturally, did not join the others who got ushered into the hallway of the little gray house. The red door closed behind them. Amy was left outside, alone outside under a lamppost on Halloween night with a real little witch girl flying back and forth amidst the ginkgo trees!

Amy put her trick or treat bag down on the sidewalk. She leaned her nonmagic broomstick against the lamppost. And she watched. Her heart beat very fast.

She told herself not to be frightened because this was

Halloween and anything might happen on Halloween, even having real witches fly up Garden Lane on broomsticks. Otherwise what was the use of Hallowen? Moreover, this little witch girl happened to be an acquaintance of hers—a friend. She watched the real little witch girl go flying low, up and down the street.

Now what was going to happen?

CHAPTER FIFTEEN

The Real Witch and the Pretend Witch

This is what happened. Little Witch Girl saw Amy, but she did not recognize her in her witch costume. She had been looking for the two girls, Amy and Clarissa, one in a pink dress and the other in a blue dress—the way they were the two other times she had seen them. Who could know that Amy was Amy behind that awful witch mask? Little Witch Girl thought Amy must be another real little witch girl, like herself, out on her saturnalia. So, she brought her broomstick down, landing neatly on the sidewalk beside the make-believe little witch, Amy.

Amy's heart beat more wildly than ever. She, of course, had recognized the little witch girl the moment she had seen her. She ought to. She had drawn her often enough. "Hi!" she said shyly.

The minute the real little witch girl heard Amy's voice, she recognized her too. She said, "Hi!" back. She was happy to have located Amy so quickly and to know that real girls dress up like witches on Halloween. "I didn't recognize you at first," she said apologetically. "I thought you always wore pink."

"That's all right," said Amy reassuringly. "If you had a

pink dress on instead of your witch clothes, I might not have reckenized you."

For a moment the two witches, real and pretend, surveyed each other silently. Then Amy said, "I wasn't sure that Old Witch would let you come."

"She didn't," said the little witch girl. "I just came."

"And Weeny Witchie?"

"She is with the little mermaid."

"Oh yes, of course," said Amy.

"Would you like to fly on my broomstick?" asked the little witch girl. "I have learned the abracadabra that will make it go for you. We just learned it in school."

Amy was overcome with joy. Ever since she had seen Little Witch Girl soaring up and down the street, she had longed to try to fly the broomstick. "Oh yes," she said.

"Thank you." Amy had often dreamed that she could fly. And although flying on a broomstick is not as important as plain flying, with only arms and legs to make you go, as in dreams, still it is quite important, she thought.

So, the real little witch girl got off the broomstick, and the pretend little witch got on. Little Witch Girl gave her broomstick a magic pat, the way one pats a pony, and she said, "Tcl, tcl." Amy was half scared and half delighted as the broomstick began to bump along the brick sidewalk, under the ginkgo trees. She was sure it left the ground.

This left the real little witch girl standing alone in the light of the lamp, without her broomstick but with her little Tommy cat in her arms. And at this moment the other children of the trick or treat expedition came trooping out of the little gray house, their bags more bulging than ever. Of course, they mistook the real little witch girl for Amy.

"Amy!" said Clarissa. "Where were you? Where did you find that cat? Go on in. Take your bag. The lady is waiting for you." And she pushed the little witch girl, whom she thought was Amy, up the steps to the red door of the little gray house, which was still wide open. The lady of the house, a very friendly lady who liked children and who did not keep their kites or balls or anything and who had baked brownies for this occasion, stood in the doorway, beckoning to the little witch girl.

She said she wanted to see this little witch girl close to and try and guess who she was. So far, she had not been able to guess who anyone was, which shows how wonderful their costumes must have been, for she knew all the children well and sometimes told them stories.

"Now, let me see," said this lady who did not confiscate balls. "Could this be . . . possibly be . . . Amy?"

The real little Halloween witch shook her head. But she said nothing lest a Halloween croak escape.

"I know you just must be Amy by your hair," said the nice lady, and she gave the little witch girl a red apple. Little Witch Girl forgot to keep silent and she croaked, "Cr-cr-cr," happily. She did not intend to put poison in one half the apple or to do anything wicked with it, even though this was Halloween. She was just going to eat it. It smelled good, being a Winesap. She took a bite, and "cr-cr-cr," she croaked happily at the juicy morsel.

"Why, Amy darling! Or whoever you are! You must have a terrible cold. Don't stay out too late. And tell your mother to rub your throat with Baume bengée when you get home."

Then she ushered the little witch girl out and closed the door, and she never found out that she had entertained a real live little witch girl in her house.

So then, while Amy was off on the broomstick, trying to get it in front of the moon, Little Witch Girl had the fun of going from house to house and getting the candies and apples and cookies, popcorn too, that were meant for Amy, the pretend witch of Garden Lane.

The real little witch girl was afraid of Christopher Knapp, the red devil, and shrank inside her cloak when he came too close to her. She was also frightened of the big pretend black cat, for Polly Knapp, swept away with enthusiasm at being a cat, kept coming at the little witch girl with her big paws, thinking, of course, this was Amy.

And Little Witch Girl was absolutely terrified of a group of little imps, ghouls, tigers, and lions who were tricksing and treating with their plain-clothes ordinary mothers. These mothers were hiding behind trees, trying to look as though they were not there, but keeping careful watch over their tiny ones. They thought the tiny ones wanted to think that they were motherless for the Halloween fun. But some of these two-year-olds were scared of themselves, and one, a tiger, said "Wah-h-h," when he saw the real little witch's face up close. Having had enough of being motherless, he fled, and his mother took him home. "There's another witch!" he screamed catching sight of Amy on the broomstick. His mother put him right to bed.

Amy was having a wonderful time with the broomstick, but she felt it really needed another little pat of magic to make it go higher. She wanted to get it in front of the moon. So, she turned it around and went back to the lamp-post where she had left the real little witch taking care of her trick or treat bag. She was going to ask Little Witch Girl to rub more magic onto the broomstick.

At this moment the children came trooping out of a house across the street from the little gray one. They were congregating again under the lamplight to decide where to go next, just as Amy came along on the broomstick. What a shame that none of the children, not even Clarissa, saw her flying! But Clarissa did see that there was one more witch here than there had been before.

"Look, Amy!" she exclaimed, tugging at the cloak of the real little witch whom she still thought was Amy despite the unusual sound of her voice. "Who's this witch?" She became all mixed up when the new little witch girl dismounted from her broomstick and stood right beside the real little witch girl whom Clarissa thought was Amy.

These two witch girls, the real one and the pretend one,

stood side by side, and no one could tell one from the other. They both had long blond hair, exactly the same, and the color of moonlight.

"Amy," said Clarissa to the wrong witch again. "Who is this new witch? Who do you think this new witch is that came up on a broomstick? Do you think it is Mary Maloney from up on Starr Street? Or maybe Sally Trout? And where did you get that cute cat?"

The two little witch girls, the real one and the pretend one, looked at each other and laughed. At first Amy had not understood why Clarissa called the other little witch, Amy, when she was Amy herself. She thought anyone would know *she* was Amy! But suddenly she caught on! Clarissa and the other children were all mixed up and still thought that Little Witch Girl was she, Amy! "She's probably gone into the houses with them," thought Amy, catching on still more. It was not surprising for the other children to get mixed up! But for her best friend, Clarissa, to get mixed up was too funny! Think of all the pictures that she and Clarissa had drawn of Little Witch Girl. And still Clarissa did not recognize the true witch! Think of the birthday party, too, the witch girl's birthday party!

"Oh, well," said Amy, excusing her. "After all. It is Halloween. Anybody can get mixed up on Halloween."

"This girl," she said slowly and solemnly to Clarissa, "is real Little Witch Girl that we draw all the time."

Clarissa looked from one to the other in utter confusion. Then she said hastily, "Why yes, of course," for she certainly recognized Amy's voice and, for the moment at least, knew that Amy was Amy.

"Please rub some more magic on that broomstick," Amy asked the real little witch girl.

Little Witch Girl shook her head. "Not in front of all the children. It doesn't work well unless we are alone."

"Later?" asked Amy.

"Maybe," said Little Witch Girl.

Polly and Christopher Knapp eyed the new witch girl (Amy) and the other witch girl (real one) suspiciously. They did not know one from the other until Amy spoke and they recognized her voice. Then they decided to be rude to the stranger witch girl who they had thought was Amy and whom they had let come into houses with them on their street on Halloween. They would pull her hair, for one thing. "You can't have that bag," said Christopher. "That's Amy's."

They had decided that this other witch was a girl from a different school, not their school. They decided she must be Mary Maloney or Sally Trout from Starr Street, both of whom had long blond hair like Amy's, unless this hair was a Halloween wig. They pulled it to see. No, it was not a wig, for it did not come off. But it crackled electrically, giving them a slight shock, so they decided to leave the new little witch girl alone. They had heard that Mary Maloney was rather a rough girl, and the shock confirmed the rumor. Anyway, they still kept getting her and Amy mixed up, and they would not want to pull the hair of Amy by mistake and get scolded by their mother who always said, "Don't pull Amy's hair!"

So, they contented themselves with singing, "Mary Maloney is full of baloney." But suddenly they stopped. There came the sound of a great whirra-whirra. The moon darkened over. "Heh-heh! Ha-ha! He-he!" The harsh laugh of the great old Halloween witch could be heard. Wind whistled. Branches of the great ginkgo trees bent low. The little make-believe hobgoblins, frightened and excited, darted hither and thither and looked real. Newspapers flew up the street and wound around the children's legs. Happily terrified, they all raced for Amy's house, where they had agreed to wind up the expedition. And in this way trick or treat ended for the year.

Little Witch Girl was just as terrified as the others. What would Old Witch do if she discovered Little Witch Girl down here on Garden Lane? Trembling, she hid under Amy's little fir tree by the front stoop. But when Amy's mother opened the front door and light spilled out and down the steps, sounds of Old Witch disappeared, and most of the children raced home. They could hardly wait to see what was in their trick and treat bags and possibly eat something.

The only children left standing in front of Amy's house were Amy, Clarissa, and the other little witch girl.

Amy's mother looked at the two little witches. "And who is this other little witchie?" she asked, having trouble recognizing her own Amy.

"Oh," said Chris Knapp's high soprano boy's voice. He was looking out of his upstairs window. "That's Mary Maloney. We know that's Mary Maloney. She can't fool us."

"S'Mary," echoed Polly Knapp quietly.

Amy's mother knew that the other witch was not Mary Maloney because she knew that Mary Maloney was a bride for this Halloween. While the children had been away tricksing and treating, Mary Maloney had come here, to the back door, with some other children from Starr Street. And Mary Maloney was not a witch. She was a bride in a long net curtain, rather torn and muddy, and she wore earrings in her ears.

"Just some other little witch from somewhere," she thought. And she thought, "This has been a very big year for witches."

"Well," said Amy's mother. "You must come in now. And this other little witch must go home. And Clarissa, your mother phoned and asked if you would like to spend the night. She is going to be home later than she thought." ("Goody! Goody!" interrupted Clarissa.) "I think you might as well both sleep in my big bed tonight." ("Oh goody, goody!" Amy interrupted.) "So come on in."

"Good-by," whispered Amy to the real little witch girl. "Thanks." And they all went in, leaving Little Witch Girl standing under the fir tree with her cat and her broomstick.

Amy and Clarissa went upstairs. In her mother's big bedroom, Amy went over to the window. The moon had gone under a cloud. When it came out, she thought she saw, in the light of it, the little witch girl down below, still standing under the fir tree.

"Little Witch Girl," she whispered. "Could Clarissa and me have one little ride? She hasn't been on the broomstick at all yet." It seemed to Amy that she heard an answering whisper, "Yes."

Amy's mother called from downstairs. "Get ready for bed now, little witchie and little Chinese girl."

"We don't have to go to bed yet," said Amy to her mother. "It's not even eight o'clock yet."

"You have had so much excitement, I think you had better," her mother said.

"We're not sleepy," said Amy.

"No," said Clarissa, yawning.

"We want to draw first," said Amy.

"Just for a little while then," said Amy's mother.

Amy and Clarissa sat down at the little yellow table. Their Halloween drawings from this morning were still there. They added a bit here and there. Their heads were nodding, but they did not want to go to bed because they were not sleepy. For just a moment Clarissa laid her head down on the table. "I'm not sleepy," she murmured.

Amy laid her head down on the other side of the table. "I'm not either," she said. "Little Witch Girl said we could have a ride, Clarissa. You and me, take turns," she said.

"I don't want a ride," said Clarissa.

"Nope!" said Amy. "You may never again, in your whole life, have a chance to ride a real broomstick."

Clarissa did not answer.

Amy's mother's voice, as from miles away, sang up the stairs. "Amy! Clarissa! Get ready for bed. In two minutes I'll be up and turn off the lights. Hurry!"

Neither little girl answered. Amy had never taken off her mask. It was not comfortable to sleep in, but she kept it on because she liked it.

"Did you hear me?" her mother said, from even farther away.

"In two minutes," murmured Amy, not raising her head from the little table. "What a two minutes this was going to be!" she thought. "Rides, broomsticks, witches . . ."

CHAPTER SIXTEEN

A Ride on a Broomstick

"Now this time," said Amy, who was rather surprised to find herself back outside, under the little fir tree, talking to the real little witch girl, "this time, please rub more magic, much more magic, onto the broomstick than you did last time, so that it will really go up into the air, not far up, just a little up. Please rub enough magic to give Clarissa and me a nice little ride back and forth on Garden Lane."

"Where is Clarissa?" asked the little witch girl.

"Oh, that's right. She doesn't like rides on merry-go-rounds and she doesn't like rides on broomsticks. So, I guess she isn't here. But hurry with the magic. We have only two minutes. Then Mama is going to put out the lights."

Little Witch Girl said, "All right." Then she said a rune. But as she was saying the rune, and Amy was straining to catch the words, there came a foreboding buzz, and Little Witch Girl received a tiny swift sting on her hand.

"THAT BE WRONG!" warned Malachi.

Alas! Too late Little Witch Girl realized she had made a mistake. In her excitement and joy over being here with Amy, under the little fir tree, she had said the wrong rune. So, the magic that she had rubbed onto the broomstick was the sort that would make it go adventuring as far and as fast as it wanted to. The broomstick, not the rider, would be the one that charted the course. Furthermore, a ride of two minutes on the broomstick might be the same as a ride of two hours, or two days, or even two years! That was the magic sort of time into which the wrong rune Little Witch Girl had said had catapulted the broomstick. The broomstick began to hop up and down from the exceedingly strong dose of magic, and Amy hopped onto it, laughing. "Gracious!" she said.

The little witch girl held it back for a moment. She did not know how to change the wrong magic that she had rubbed onto it. Magic that is very hard to learn cannot be erased in a second. However, in a desperate effort to change it, Little Witch Girl tucked the Malachi rune into the hem of Amy's witch cloak.

"What's that for?" asked Amy as the broomstick left the ground.

"To use in case of gravest trouble," shouted Little Witch Girl.

"I BE WITH YOU!" spelled Malachi.

It was a comforting voice to hear as Amy shot straight up in the air like a skyrocket. She held on tightly, and she knew that she would come back eventually because of gravity, magic or not. So, she did not worry about anything except that she hoped the ride would not go over two minutes, that was all. She had to be back at her little table when Mama came up to turn off the lights.

Amy enjoyed the ride. As she shot along, she took in the sights. She saw many real witches flying around, and she was glad she had kept her witch false face on so she could not be distinguished from them. The witches were at their saturnalia, and she joined in on the outskirts for a while,

doing pinwheels and then flying on. Amy had not one thing to do about whether she and the broomstick would join in or not. The broomstick decided all.

Once Amy became frightened and her heart beat loudly when she saw the real old witch at one hurly-burly. Old Witch exclaimed right in her ear, "Oh, to glory be!" and, "Heh-heh, great fun isn't it?" But Old Witch was too full of the glory of being herself and of attracting a great deal of attention to notice that Amy was not a real little witch girl. If Old Witch had recognized her banquisher, goodness knows what might have happened! "It's lucky I have on a disguise," thought Amy.

"Oh, wicked, wicked me!" Old Witch sang gleefully. Then, followed by some bats and some imps, she went on with her swooping. And Amy went on, on her broomstick.

Then a lucky thing happened for Amy or she might have been carried up to the moon. The broomstick, being small and tender, had grown tired. Happening to glimpse Old Witch's abode on top of the bare, barren, bleak glass hill, it resolved to stay there.

"Probably," thought Amy, half exasperated and half amused, "it's saying, 'I've had enough. I want to go to bed.' It doesn't ask *me* what *I* want. I'd like to go to bed too." No matter how much Amy tried to persuade the broomstick to go again, and this time down—she hoped—it would not comply. It swept itself over to its comfortable corner in Old Witch's house and it stayed there.

And there, in Old Witch's house, Amy had to stay too.

She was stranded in the home of the witch family on top of the bare and bleak glass hill, and she had no way of getting home except by means of the broomstick, which would not take her there. Down below, on beautiful Garden Lane, Mama was probably worrying about her. Amy did not realize that not even a minute had gone by down there and that Mama had not yet gone upstairs to turn off the lights and tuck her and Clarissa in bed.

First Amy went to find Malachi. There he was, looking pale green in the bright moonlight. "I be here," said Amy to him.

"YES, YOU BE!" he said—a short sentence, but all that was necessary.

Then Amy sat down in Little Witch Girl's red rocker, which was just like her own, and she rocked back and forth, back and forth. She wondered how she was going to get home; and she wondered about Little Witch Girl— what plight *she* might be in without her broomstick. Looking about in the moonlight, Amy thought how awfully bare and bleak this glass hill was that she had thought up! Not a tree! One might as well be on the moon, the cold moon.

Perhaps Amy should fix it so that Old Witch, now that she was good ("Of course, I know she *is* good," Amy said to herself comfortingly.), would not have to live in such bare emptiness any more. It must be very gloomy for her and for the little witch girl. For Weeny Witchie, too. It must.

And right now, it was also gloomy for Amy. Oh, to be home in bed! Amy was tired of Halloween. Back and forth and back and forth she rocked. She tried not to think what Old Witch would do to her when she came home and found her here. She hoped that Old Witch would have spent all her wickedness by then and that she would not try to eat her up like the old witch tried to in "Hansel and Gretel." "If only at least I had a brother here to help push Old Witch in the oven." Or if only Clarissa, her best friend, were here too.

Oh, dear! If only dear Clarissa *were* here with her! It is ever so much pleasanter to be in a witch house with your best friend than by yourself. The day of Little Witch Girl's party she and Clarissa had had quite a good time here! A happy thought struck Amy. Perhaps as at that party, she would be invisible to Old Witch. Since she was not invisible to herself, she had no way of knowing whether she would be invisible to Old Witch or not. Maybe she should not wait to find out. Maybe she should hide. But where? It was all so shiny up here, and no trees. Maybe she'd better get into Little Witch Girl's bed and pull the covers up over her head and pretend that she was real little witch girl, sound asleep. This seemed like a very good idea, especially as she heard Malachi spell approvingly, "G o o d!"

So, Amy courageously tiptoed into the dark witch house and crawled into the brass bed and pulled the black bed-clothes up over her head. But she did not like it here at all. If only she were at home, at her little yellow table with Clarissa, drawing! That was the safest spot that she knew of. But she wasn't, alas, she was here. Naturally, she was worried about Old Witch. "Anybody would be," she assured herself. She felt of the little wad of paper the little witch girl had tucked into the hem of her cloak. "In case of gravest trouble," Little Witch Girl had said.

"Well, this isn't trouble at all," said Amy to reassure herself. She was just in a witch house. That wasn't trouble, was it? "Dear Old Witchie isn't going to eat me up. I'm like Daddy," she mused. "I like adventure. This *is* adventure."

All she had to do was wait for Old Witch to come home, take off her shoes, and go to sleep. Then she must outwit her. This much Amy had learned from stories like "Molly Whuppie."

Now and then, to get a breath, Amy peeked out from under the bedclothes. Sometimes the moon, coming out from behind a cloud, shone brightly through the window and onto the little witch girl's bed where Amy lay pondering what to do. The moon seemed to say to her, "I am your friend from Garden Lane." Still, Amy felt lonesome. Two things that she would like most of all in the world right now would be to have Mama tucking her in bed and saying, "Sweet my Amy." The next best would be to have Clarissa here.

Amy turned over. It is not comfortable to be in bed under the bedclothes in a witch costume including the tall witch hat and the mask. Then, tired out, and still thinking of a way to outwit Old Witch when she came home, Amy fell asleep in the witch house with her witch mask on.

But the eyes of Malachi the bumblebee remained wide open and alert. "I BE HERE! I BE HERE!" he spelled over and over again, and he kept up a gentle sort of humming and buzzing all night long. This was intended to be reassuring to Amy in case she should wake up and feel afraid. Hearing him, she would be able to think, "Ah, there's Malachi."

CHAPTER SEVENTEEN

Malachi, to the Rescue

When Amy waked up, the moon was gone and the sun was shining. Halloween was over. Yet here she was, still up here in the witch house! How she longed to be home, even having oatmeal, of which she was not very fond, for breakfast. Her mask was all bent and crooked. Straightening it out, she peeked over to Old Witch's bed. Why, for heaven's sake! Old Witch wasn't home yet. Her saturnalia must go on all night and into the next day, luckily for Amy.

Determined to go, somehow or another, before Old Witch did return and see her here in the plain light of day, Amy took the broomstick out onto the rickety front porch and stood it up straight. She thought that the broomstick should take her home, now that morning had come. She thought it must miss the real little witch girl and be tired of a pretend one in a witch disguise. It stood up nicely all by itself. Before getting on, however, Amy tiptoed over to Malachi's sunny corner to make sure he was still there. He was. And he was looking huge, puffed out, and golden in the glinting autumn sunshine. Amy felt the hem of her cloak for the paper that Little Witch Girl had tucked there. It crinkled cosily.

"Malachi," said Amy.

"Y E S," spelled Malachi.

"I have a paper that I may use in gravest trouble," said Amy.

"Y E S," spelled Malachi.

"But I am not in gravest trouble. At least I don't think I am," she said.

"A MATTER OF OPINION," spelled Malachi

"That is what I thought," said Amy who really did not know what OPINION spelled. "And, Malachi, please don't use too hard words, please."

"N O," said Malachi.

"That's better," said Amy. "Good-by. You are the best representatiff I ever had." Blowing him a kiss, she flung her legs over the broomstick.

"Go," said Amy, and "G O," she spelled to make it more emphatic. "Please take me home."

The broomstick did go. Off it flew. But it did not fly her home. Amy's messenger, the red cardinal bird, happened to be flying by just then, and from habit the broomstick followed after him. So it was that the broomstick carried Amy to the witch school. At the little pink cloud, the broomstick left the bird, flew in the window of the witch school, where Amy, with pounding heart, dismounted. To give herself courage, she felt the hem of her cloak to be sure the paper was safe.

The other little witches had apparently just arrived. They were breathless still, and they were yawning and complaining that they were worn out from the best Halloween there ever had been. Old Witch had surpassed herself, they said. They were all so tired and sleepy that they did not recognize Amy as Amy. She had kept her witch mask on, of course, and this helped. The little witches thought Amy was Hannah. They clustered around her and began to compare notes as to who had had the greatest Halloween hurly-burly.

"What did you do, Hannah?" asked Tweet.

They all supposed that since Hannah lived with the real great old witch, the head witch of all witches, she had had the most exciting time of any of them. Luckily just then the witch teacher said, "Attention," so Amy did not have to reply.

First the teacher read the roll call. Amy remembered to say, "There," when the name of Hannah was called. She remembered that witches often say the opposite, for instance "there" for "here," and in this case "there" was the right answer.

But unfortunately, Amy was the first one called upon in witchiplication, and she got every answer wrong. This is not surprising, since no subject is harder for a real, ordinary girl. But her answers were a surprise to the witch teacher, because usually Little Witch Girl got the answers all right. Being in a holiday frame of mind, the teacher, though surprised, did not mark her down.

But when in arithmetic Amy, from habit, said, "One and one is two," instead of "One and one is nothing," she received terrible marks and had to learn nine hard runes by heart for punishment. Opening the little witch girl's notebook, she had a pleasant surprise. In the little witch girl's handwriting, which was very fine and resembled the delicate marks of sandpipers in the sand, but which Amy could read quite well, she found the following broomstick rune:

> Down-ee, down-ee, down we go
> Down the big glass hill we go.

> In sun, in rain, in sleet, in snow
> Down to Garden Lane we go.

This was an easy rune for Amy to learn, and she learned it in a second. At the first opportunity she was going to try it on the broomstick. The broomstick was still so full of the powerful magic that the little witch girl had patted onto it that instead of standing sedately in the corner with the other broomsticks, it kept hopping up and down.

"Can't you quiet that restless broomstick of yours?" the witch teacher asked Amy, still thinking that Amy was Hannah.

Here was Amy's chance. The broomstick was so restless that it would probably take her home now, especially when it heard the rune she had just learned.

"Take it out for a little airing around the schoolhouse," suggested the witch teacher. "It's too distracting."

"Pet!" muttered the other little witches jealously.

Amy was overjoyed. But alas! Her joy was short-lived. As she left her desk, an awful thing happened. Her witch mask fell off, and before she could slap it back on, who should glimpse her real little girl's face but Itch and Twitch, the twins.

"That is not Hannah!" they screamed. "That is a spy! That is the banquisher of witches to glass hills. Catch her! Catch her!"

The little witches fell upon Amy. They tied her arms and legs with strong spider-web silk, and they put her in the corner. The witch teacher came and stared at her and said, just like real Old Witch, "Oh, to glory be!"

In this way Amy became a captive of the little witches. There she was imprisoned in a silken spider web in a corner of the witch schoolroom. "The trouble be grave now," she

said to herself. "I do not think it be of the gravest, though."
Amy wondered if she should wait for it to become gravest.
She held tightly to the corner of the hem of her cloak, and
clutched the paper folded there in readiness lest grave became gravest all of a sudden.

It did. The little witches all got out their witchiplication
books and sat in a semicircle around Amy. "We'll change
her into a rabbit," they said, and they pored over the books
to find the proper rune for changing real little girls into
rabbits. "Rabbits, rabbits, rabbits," they muttered. "Changing girls into rabbits. . . . She shall be a present to Old
Witch," they said, "as a reward for conducting the best
Halloween ever, and as a consolation prize for losing the
spelling bee."

"Ha!" said Olie. "I have it!"

All the little witches stood up. Olie read:

> "Oh girl, tied up in the webs of a spider,
>   Old Witchie would like to have ye inside her.
>   We'll soon change ye into a rabbit
>   And send ye off—it is our habit—
>   To be a gift to our Old Witch
>   Than whom there is none better than which.
>   On thy bones Old Witch will gnaw
>   As soon as thy toes become a—paw!"

The witches then entered into frightening backanallies.
And, one, two, three, stomp! They came stomping along,
faster and faster, one, two, three, stomp! One, two, three,
stomp! And, "Tweak the nose, and tweak the chin," they
sang, "Until they bend out instead of bend in."

This ceremony was a nightmare to Amy. This was gravest trouble, all right, she decided. She got the piece of paper

out from the hem of her cloak, unfolded it, and quickly
read:

> "Malachi!
> Oh, Malachi!
> You are a magic bumblebee
> You are the
> spelling bumblebee.
> And if in trouble
> e'er I be
> Then mumble
> bumble
> here to me!"

Malachi came!

He flew through the open window, looking tremendous. "TAKE HEED! TAKE HEED!" he buzzed as he darted through the stomping witches, giving each one a big, big bite. "BEWARE!" he said.

"Teacher," the little witch girls whimpered, falling back.

With this Amy broke the silken cords that bound her. She had known all along one thing that little witches do not know, and that is that although little witches cannot break the silken webs of spiders when they are bound with them, real little girls can. She had not broken them before because she had to have a friend at hand to help her to escape.

Malachi alighted in front of Amy, his wings fluttering. His buzzing boded ill. He seemed to be growing larger all the time. All the witches fell back to the wall, watching and listening. Without turning around to look at them (by tilting his head back he could see them anyway from his top center eye), Malachi spelled, "GOOD WILL WIN!"

"Malachi?" Amy said.

"YES," he spelled.

"It was of the gravest, I think," she said.

"MAYBE!" he spelled.

"Now that you be here, everything be all right," said Amy. "Malachi?" she said.

"YES," he replied in the spelling fashion. The little witches followed the conversation with rapt attention even though he was spelling forward and not backward.

"Be it not true that a bumblebee can carry objects of much greater weight than itself? My father told me that once."

"TRUE," said Malachi.

"So. A bumblebee be stronger than an elephant because an elephant cannot do that?"

"T R U E," said Malachi, puffing out his plushlike back.

"Then," said Amy happily, "it will not be hard for you to fly me home, will it? This broomstick will not go where I say. And I must get it back to the little witch girl."

Malachi said, "S O B E I T!"

Then he swelled himself out tremendously. He looked as big as the sun. He almost blinded the witches' eyes. Then great Malachi, puffing himself out still more mightily, said, "G E T O N!"

Clutching Little Witch Girl's broomstick tightly to her, Amy climbed up onto Malachi's soft, furry back.

Then Malachi fluttered his great beautiful gossamer wings, rose into the air, and away he flew out the window with Amy!

The little witch girls crowded together in astonishment at the window as they witnessed this extraordinary flight of a bumblebee. Then, recovering themselves, they hopped onto their broomsticks and, crying, "Yup-giddy, yup-giddy!" they gave chase. It was quite a spectacle to see them, like a flock of birds, flying in formation, with the twins on their twin-broomstick in the lead. But, outdistanced in no time, they had to give up the chase and fly away back to witch school, where they compared bites.

As Malachi and Amy flew past the secret opening into the glass hill that led to the mermaid lagoon, Amy thought she heard a far and distant wailing. "Wah, wah, wah!" she heard.

"Ah," murmured Amy. "Weeny baby witchie! Don't cry, Beebee," she called to it. "Sister will come for you soon."

Then a strange thing happened. Though it had been morning just now when they had left the witch school, the farther down they flew, the darker and darker it became. Soon it was night. They went so fast that Malachi looked like a golden meteor to the little witch girl who was waiting under the little fir tree. She had not stirred from this spot—the two minutes just coming to an end for her.

Malachi dipped down so that Amy could give the little witch girl her broomstick. "I . . . I . . ." said Amy. She was all confused. She wanted to tell Little Witch Girl her adventures, but they were beginning to get as blurry in her mind as the form of Malachi, in the dark, was. Then Malachi flew Amy through the open window of her mother's big bedroom and deposited her at the little yellow table. And then Malachi and the real little witch girl, on her broomstick again, flew away and away and back to the glass hill, leaving Amy, pretend witch, asleep at the little yellow table, opposite Clarissa, little pretend Chinese girl.

Mama came up to put out the lights. The long two minutes were over. "Ts, ts, ts," Mama said, "they're sound asleep." She laid them on the big bed, not undressing them, for she did not want to wake them up. Saying, "Sweet my Amy," she took her battered witch mask and witch hat off, looked long into the radiant face, and kissed her on the rounded top of her little blond head. Those two minutes had been as any other two minutes to Mama. She did not know that the extra radiance that shone on Amy's face was from the two great rides she had had, one on a broomstick, the other on golden Malachi.

Little Witch Girl, having picked up Beebee in the mermaid lagoon, was getting into her little brass bed now, too. Thoughts of the Halloween happenings on Garden Lane were floating through her head, as they were floating through Amy's dreams also.

Malachi was back now in his camouflage place at the end of the porch. "HALLOWEEN BE OVER!" he thought. He spelled his thoughts as well as his talk.

CHAPTER EIGHTEEN

Grass!

The next day Amy and Clarissa were sitting at the little yellow table, drawing and coloring. Clarissa had already forgotten almost all about the extra little witch girl who had joined the Halloween doings on their street. After all, Clarissa, not having had the urge to get on a broomstick, had not become as mixed up with the witches as Amy had. Naturally, if you are dressed up as a little Chinese girl, you are less tempted to ride on a broomstick than if you are dressed up as a witch.

However, Amy happily reminded Clarissa of events and filled in the gaps of the story for her.

"Draw me tied up in the spider webs," Amy instructed her.

"Was there a spider in with you?" asked Clarissa in her high little voice. She was trying to draw spider webs around Amy, the pretend witch, and there was room for a spider.

"Oh, I hope not," said Amy, shuddering. "But . . . there might have been. Yes. There was probably an enormous black widow one. I think there was, Clarissa. Draw it!"

Amy pushed back her chair. She looked at the picture she was drawing. "There I am," she said fondly, "on Malachi." Then she looked wonderingly at her tall little peaked witch hat that was lying on her mother's big bed. She gave a happy sigh. What a Halloween it had been! How could she wait a whole year for the next one? But how glad she was that she was Amy and not a real little witch. And how glad she was that she lived on Garden Lane, the most beautiful street in the world, and not up on the awful bare and bleak glass hill. Poor little witch girl, to have to live up there!

Amy put her witch hat on and, standing on tiptoes, she looked at herself in the mirror above the mantel. She pressed her nose down and her chin up with her fingers. She had discovered lately that when you try to make your face look like someone else's, you may get a clue as to what that person is like inside. Right now, trying to look like Little Witch Girl, she felt pathetic. Brave and staunch and bright as Little Witch Girl was, nevertheless she was pathetic.

"IT BE BARE UP HERE!" a voice seemed to buzz.

"I know," said Amy with a sigh. "I know."

Amy thought about the bare and bleak glass hill. To think that that was where Little Witch Girl and Weeny Witchie had to live! And that Amy had thought it up! It was all right for Old Witch to live there. But Little Witch Girl? And Beebee? And Malachi?

Probably Old Witch was still asleep right this minute, tired out from her saturnalia. "Make Old Witch still asleep and snoring," she instructed Clarissa. "You know how to draw snores? Lots of z's, that's how."

"I know," said Clarissa, snoring some loud pretend snores.

"I said, 'Draw them,' not 'Snore them,'" said Amy.

They both laughed at this smart thing to say. Then Amy grew sober again, thinking about the little witch girl. Right now, Little Witch Girl was probably all alone on her rickety old front porch, lonesome, and thinking about Halloween and about Garden Lane. And about the wind rustling in the trees and the fall flowers swaying, and about the pretty pumpkins in the windows, and the children in their bright costumes under the lamplight, playing. Of the candles, too, lighted on the table, and of everything being warm.

"THERE BE NO GRASS UP HERE!" Amy seemed to hear the reproachful voice.

"No falling leaves," said Amy.

"THERE BE NO FLOWERS."

"There should be a flower," said Amy.

And she said to herself, "After all, Little Witch Girl and Beebee were not the wicked ones. It was old great-great-great-great-great-grandmother Old Witch who was the mean and wicked one. Grass! Why shouldn't I make grass grow? Think of Witchie Baby rolling in the grass! Besides, even Old Witch is good now. She didn't eat any real rabbits, and she didn't eat me. She didn't eat up anybody for a Halloween treat. I don't think she did."

"Draw grass!" she instructed Clarissa, getting back to her own drawing and starting to draw feverishly. She kept her witch hat on in order to draw better. "They need to roll in the grass. Draw flowers, too," she added.

"What!" said Clarissa incredulously. Her high little voice grew higher. "Grass! Flowers! On the bare glass hill?"

"Yes," said Amy. "I'm making the grass to grow there now. And flowers and . . . you'll see. First I'll write a letter."

Amy wrote the letter to the little witch girl who received it about a half an hour later by courtesy of the messenger cardinal. He dropped it into her lap as she sat rocking, lonesomely, in her red rocker on the rickety front porch.

"Oh!" Little Witch Girl exclaimed joyously. This was the third time that she had had a letter from Amy when she was feeling very, very lonesome. The letter was short and it said:

> "Dear Little Witch Girl,
>   Happy, happy me
> and happy, happy you.
> Look all around and round
> about.
>   I love you and you
> love me,
>   Amy."

Little Witch Girl stopped rocking and she looked all about. What was happening? Grass was growing! The glass hill was turning into a regular, ordinary grass hill! Some glass melted into a little pool with lovely trees around it right in front of Old Witch's porch. Waterfalls could be heard trickling down the mountainside. Flowers, lovely flowers, burst into bloom all over. It did not matter that this was November now. Flowers were springing up everywhere. The hill was covered with star grass. Butterflies and dragonflies darted about.

Little Witch Girl stepped off the porch. It was a strange feeling not to slip. She turned and looked at the house. It had become a pretty little white house. Roses spread over the roof, and on the porch honeysuckle blossomed. At the end of the porch, near Malachi's place, there was a green swing, the kind suspended by chains and springs and covered with an awning. Malachi, himself, had come out of his camouflage hiding place and alighted on a pink clover near the pool. It was his favorite flower.

"s w e e t!" he spelled.

Little Witch Girl spread her arms out wide in joy. "Oh, thank you, thank you," she breathed. She ran indoors and got Beebee to show her the sights.

Beebee said, "Abra, abra, abra," and sent some sparks out over the pool she was so dazzled at the glinting of the sun on the ripples.

The little witch girl said, "This can be our swimming pool. I think witches can swim in witch swimming pools, though not in any other kind. Maybe the little mermaid can come up here and visit me now and bring Babay with her. What will she think of this pool, out in the sunshine? I wonder if she has flowers, real ones, in the lagoon now, too."

As if in answer to her thoughts, who should appear from the depths of the pool but the little mermaid with Babay on her back! The mermaid cow next emerged and, uttering a questioning moo, she flopped herself up onto the star grass at the edge. Little Witch Girl was rather frightened of the cow, for this was the first time she had seen her. But she grew accustomed to Moolly, and after a while took rides on her back in the pool.

"How did you ever get up here?" Little Witch Girl asked the mermaid. "I thought I would have to get you here by abracadabra."

"There's a secret stream," said the little mermaid.

"There're flowers along beside it. There're flowers everywhere, all of a sudden, real ones; the glass ones have become real."

"They have!" said Little Witch Girl. "Imagine real flowers inside of a glass hill. My!"

Now the little mermaid could come and visit her here and play in her pool sometimes. And sometimes she could abracadabra a little boat for herself and sail down the secret stream in it and visit the little mermaid at her pool and see the flowers there—take turns.

"Do you know what I am going to do?" she said to the little mermaid. "I am going in swimming with you. This is a witch pool and it is all right for witches to swim in it."

The little mermaid climbed quickly out of the pool onto an emerald green rock, where she had placed Babay. "Will I turn into a water witch? I don't want to turn into a water

witch. Just a plain ordinary mermaid—that is what I want to stay."

"No," said the little witch decidedly. "You won't turn into a water witch or any kind of witch. "I don't thi-ink you will. Because you do not have on a witch hat."

This seemed sensible, and the little mermaid slid back into the pool. Little Witch Girl made ready to take the plunge, too. Then she thought she'd better swim in her underwear—long black tights and black shirt. This costume looked like an old-fashioned bathing suit, the way Amy had drawn it, and did nicely for the pool.

After their swim the little witch girl and the little mermaid lay on the rock beside the babies and basked in the golden sunshine. Moolly, the cow, lay on the other side of the pool, where daisies and buttercups had appeared, placidly chewing her cud. One would think, to hear her moo, that one was on a farm.

Filled with happiness, the little witch girl looked all about her. More and more flowers were bursting into blossom. An apple tree appeared, aglow with delicate pink blossoms. Weeping willow trees and other kinds of trees appeared in appropriate places. Herbs of all descriptions, easy to find ones and hard to find ones, filled the air with spicy fragrance. The old witch house, white now, seemed like a dream house high in the clouds.

Now Little Witch Girl had everything—a baby witch sister, a most-important-of-all-witches witch grandmother, and a best friend, the little mermaid from the mermaid lagoon. Moreover, she had another wonderful friend, Amy, who sent her important letters with beautiful surprises in them. All these letters she kept under her pillow, tied with Beebee's pink bootee ribbon. Beebee, being witch, did not want anything pink on her and kept throwing the pink ribbon away. But Little Witch Girl liked it and kept it for the letters. And it was this letter writer, this real girl named Amy and of the age of seven—now—who had made everything good happen.

"Moo-oo!" said the mermaid cow, echoing her contentment.

This moo apparently aroused Old Witch from her long after-saturnalia sleep. When she saw all the beauty laid out before her, she gave a great, throaty croak. "Oh, to glory be!" she muttered, and she sank into her rocker, taking in one thing and then another.

It is hard to believe, but it was true, that an old witch of her great reputation could have become so good that she enjoyed the beauty of the scene and did not pine for bats and caves and briers and brambles instead. It must be said that, for a moment, however, when Old Witch saw the mermaids, thoughts of fishing rods flashed into her mind. But the mermaids were so interesting, sporting in the sunshine, she decided to—

"LET THEM BE!" A sharply admonishing voice hummed in her ear.

"Oh, certainly," Old Witch said hastily. "Oh, to glory be! That bee still be here!" she muttered. Bemused, Old Witch rocked and rocked in her wicker rocker, which had not changed into a chaise longue or anything else that is fancy. Amy knew how fond Old Witch was of this rocker the way it was; and it still creaked pleasantly as it used to before the transformation on the glass hill had taken place, sounding the way an old front porch wicker rocker should.

As the old witch sat and rocked, she thought, "This be a witch's—a bad good witch's paradise. Oh, to glory be!

Heh-heh!" She didn't know whether to be glad or angry. "What did I do to bring this about?" she asked aloud.

"NOTHING!" spelled a voice. "ALL BE DONE BY AMY!"

Down on Garden Lane Amy and Clarissa had finished their drawings. "I've drawn so many flowers my arm is falling off," said Amy complacently. She looked long and happily at her drawing.

Old Witch was smelling a pink rose, and the little witch girl was holding a bunch of flowers so large that the flowers were spilling out of her fingers and down the mountainside. In the middle of softest, silkiest rose petals, the little witch baby was kicking her bare feet and making sparks fly through her fingers. She was cooing gently, gurgling to herself in great happiness. The mermaids had garlands in their hair. The red cardinal bird had alighted in the weeping willow tree, thoughtfully considering a nest. A little rabbit was peeking over the top of the hill. This was Brave Jack, hero of the day of the raid on the painting field. Jack was here on a scouting expedition to see how things stood with Old Witch these days. Never before would he have come up here, for the hill had been too slippery, and anyway why come to the place of exile of wicked Old Witch? But now, all was grass. Though his bright eyes never left Old Witch, his twitching nose took in the unusualness of the foliage up here. He would have much to report to Head Rabbit, who was busy below in the painting field. The three cats, big, medium, and little, were lined up at the edge of the pool, looking at themselves in it and cleaning their paws. Malachi was inside a honeysuckle blossom, arranging for a new place of camouflage and cleaning his feelers. Bees clean themselves even more than cats.

Clarissa surveyed Amy's picture for a long time. "She was good ever after, wasn't she?" she said after a while.

"Who was good ever after?" demanded Amy sternly.

"Old Witch," said Clarissa.

"What!" said Amy. "Wicked old mean Old Witch? Good ever after? Clarissa, are you a nope? Of course, she wasn't. She was still awful sometimes. The rest of the time she was good. Only when she was awful she was not good. Clarissa, listen to me. She *is* Old Witch, isn't she? What is the good of Old Witch if she is good all the time?"

Clarissa was confused. She gave a quizzical little laugh. "I don't know," she said.

"She can still be bad for Halloween, can't she? But not too bad. Just bad enough," said Amy. "I'm leaving Malachi right up there, I am. As my representatiff. See? There he is in the honeysuckle."

"Pretty big," said Clarissa.

"He *is* big," said Amy.

And that is the way things were, with the witch family now.

"Lunchtime!" Amy's mother called up the stairs.

Clarissa was having lunch with Amy today. They were having lamb chops. In this house there were almost always lamb chops for lunch, just as at Clarissa's it was usually long 'noodoos.'

The girls sat down. Amy's mother cut the meat off the bone for them, and so they began on the bone. "Tell a story about Old Witch," said Amy. "Make it bad, but not too bad. Have it begin bad, but end good. All right, begin. One day, Old Witch . . ."

At this moment there was a buzzing and a scratching at the windowpane. Malachi! His eyes looked wild and foreboding. The window was open a little, so Amy could hear what he spelled.

"A P P L E S," he spelled.

Amy looked at Clarissa. "Oh-h-h," she gasped, and she clasped her hands over her mouth. "I should not have had an apple tree to grow. You know why . . ."

"P O I S O N!" spelled Malachi.

"Yes," said Amy. "Poison. She can put poison in the halves of the apples!" Then Amy recovered her composure. "Oh, that's all right," she said reassuringly. "Maybe the blossoms will not turn into apples. Or maybe just one apple will grow. That's all right, isn't it, Clarissa, for there to be one apple for Old Witch to put poison in one half of it?"

"Oh yes, of course," said Clarissa.

Malachi, gravely humming, flew away to his new camouflage place on Old Witch's porch in the white and golden honeysuckle.

"Well, come on," said Amy to her mother. "Come on. *Bee*gin. One day, Old Witch . . ."

Books by Eleanor Estes
available in paperback editions
from Harcourt Brace Jovanovich, Inc.

THE MOFFATS

THE MIDDLE MOFFAT

THE HUNDRED DRESSES

GINGER PYE

PINKY PYE

THE WITCH FAMILY